SURF

Amanda picked u
Supply. The lid popped open and several bottles of Wite-Out rolled onto the ground. One of them was smashed and covered her in white powder as she picked it up.

"Oh, great. Now I'm going to get this stuff all over the inside of my bag." She reached down and touched the white powder. "It's all dried up. What a lousy product."

Mick knelt soundlessly beside her and held the remains of the broken bottle in his hand.

"Amanda."

Something in Mick's voice made her freeze. "What is it?"

Mick looked over both shoulders and then down at his hands. "I think I just figured out why those hoods are after me."

"Why?"

"This isn't Wite-Out," Mick said quietly. "It's cocaine."

Titles available in the HART AND SOUL series, published by Bantam Books:

1. KILL THE STORY
2. PLAY DEAD
3. SPEAK NO EVIL
4. GET THE PICTURE
5. TOO HOT TO HANDLE
6. SIGNED, SEALED, DELIVERED

HART AND SOUL 6

SIGNED, SEALED, DELIVERED

JAHNNA N. MALCOLM

BANTAM BOOKS
NEW YORK • TORONTO • LONDON • SYDNEY • AUCKLAND

SIGNED, SEALED, DELIVERED

A BANTAM BOOK 0 553 17626 9

First published in USA by Bantam Books, a division of Bantam Doubleday Dell Publishing Group, Inc.

First publication in Great Britain

PRINTING HISTORY
Bantam edition published 1992

Bantam Books are published by Transworld Publishers Ltd., 61-63 Uxbridge Road, Ealing, London W5 5SA, in Australia by Transworld Publishers (Australia) Pty. Ltd., 15-23 Helles Avenue, Moorebank, NSW 2170, and in New Zealand by Transworld Publishers (N.Z.) Ltd., Cnr. Moselle and Waipareira Avenues, Henderson, Auckland.

Made and printed in Great Britain by
BPCC Hazell Books
Aylesbury, Bucks, England
Member of BPCC Ltd.

This book is gratefully dedicated
to
Dr. Carl J. Harms,
for bringing us our special delivery,
Dashiell McLean,
born March 22, 1989

CHAPTER ONE

"Fleet Street. Talk to me."

Mickey Soul cradled the phone beneath his ear as he paced back and forth beside his battered desk. It was early Monday morning—the beginning of a new week at his San Francisco messenger service—and things were off to a shaky start. Mick winced at the sharp tone of the caller.

"Yes, I know we haven't gotten a rider over to your office yet," he said, pushing a fallen lock of his dark hair off his forehead. "We're shorthanded this morning."

The light bulb hanging down from the ceiling cast a harsh glare across the room. A threadbare couch and an overstuffed armchair had been pushed up against the wall to one side of the door. On the other side a row of red metal lockers leaned against the wall. Two riders who were adjusting their ten-speeds in the corner suddenly burst into laughter.

"Just a minute." Mick covered the mouthpiece with his hand and shouted, "Hey, you guys, I can't hear myself think." He turned back to the phone. "Just cool your jets, lady, okay? We'll have someone out there as soon as we can." He hung up and yelled loudly, "Gabe? Where are you, anyway?"

As if on cue, the door behind him opened and a stocky teen stepped into the room. Gabriel Sanchez was Mick's partner and best friend. Today he looked tired and rumpled. He flung his bag onto the desk. "Sorry, man, I overslept."

"That's okay." Mick patted him on the shoulder. "But we've got to hustle and get these riders on the streets."

The phone rang and Gabe scooped it up. Mick grabbed several yellow forms and quickly sorted them in order. "Phil," he called, "you're up first."

Phil Wilayto jogged across the room to the desk. He wore a Greenpeace T-shirt tucked into a pair of oversize red sweats. A Giants baseball cap was turned backward on his head. Mick looked at his tiger-striped high-tops and winced. "You could be cited for visual assault with that rig. Ever hear of good taste?"

Phil ignored the jibe and said, "What've you got for me?"

Mick thrust several of the yellow slips of paper

into the bike rider's hand. "Here's your first set of dispatches. They're all in the same area near Market and Montgomery so you should be able to cover them in one sweep."

Phil took the sheaf of papers, then lowered his voice and said, "Hey, Mick, I need to talk to you."

"Later, Phil, okay?" Mick replied, busily sorting out the remaining orders as Gabe stuffed another handful in front of him. "We're going nuts here."

"But I really—"

"Later, man."

The phone rang again and Gabe barked into the receiver, "Fleet Street."

As Mick watched Phil leave, he rubbed his temple, where a headache was already starting to form. "Where's Tyrone?"

"He's not coming in," Gabe called, covering the receiver with his hand. "He said he still can't ride because of that ankle he sprained last week."

"Oh, great, that's all we need," Mick muttered. "We're already short because of Terry Han going on vacation, my no-good cousin hasn't bothered to show up today, and now Tyrone's out." He faced his friend. "You and I are going to have to pick up all the slack around here."

Gabe hung up the phone, shaking his head. "It's gonna be a long day. The Clifford Agency wants to know why we haven't got a pickup at their office yet. They're pretty tweaked. Mr. Alvarson says he's going to use another messenger service."

"I hate Mondays." Mick turned in his chair and shouted, "Hey, Cynthia!"

"That's my name. Don't wear it out."

Mick smiled at the slightly built figure who stepped up to the desk, carrying a worn bike helmet under her arm. Cynthia Spartaro was only five feet tall but an absolute spitfire on a bicycle.

"I need your help."

"Whatever you've got, I can handle it."

Cynthia's boyish features were accentuated by an impish upturned nose that matched her feisty nature. She pulled her thick brown hair into a ponytail and shoved it up under her cap.

"Head over to the Clifford Agency *pronto* and give them my sincerest apologies. Oh, and Cyn—lay it on thick."

Cynthia batted her eyelashes at Mick. "Like this?"

He chuckled. "That'll do."

After she left, the phone rang again.

"Looks like this one's for me," Mick declared as he wrote down the address on a yellow invoice. He unlocked his bike from the rack outside and headed for the street.

Suddenly a black sedan pulled into the alley, blocking his exit. Mick slammed on his brakes and scraped his shoulder against the brick wall as he tried to slip by the car. "Watch it!" Mick shouted angrily.

The passenger door opened abruptly and banged right into Mick, knocking him off the ten-speed.

Before he knew what was happening, two men leaped out of the car and shoved him roughly up against the wall.

"This is a warning, punk," one of them growled. "You're in the wrong business."

"What are you talking about?" Mick protested.

One of the men punched him hard in the stomach. The pain was so intense Mick saw stars. He gasped for breath and slowly slid to his knees.

"Shut it down by midnight Thursday," the other man rasped, "or we'll shut you down—permanently."

CHAPTER TWO

"Ow!" Mick jerked his head back out of Gabe's reach. "What're you trying to do, kill me?"

Gabe grunted and stopped dabbing the cut on Mick's forehead with a cotton ball. "I thought you said they only hit you once—in the stomach."

"Right." Mick winced as he gingerly felt the rising bump on his temple. "This is where my head hit the pavement when I fell."

"Well, you're gonna live," Gabe declared, setting the bottle of antiseptic down on the desk. "Tell me once again what those clowns looked like."

Mick leaned back in the desk chair and heaved an exhausted sigh. "There were two of them, about medium height, medium build, both wearing hats, overcoats, black gloves."

"That really tells us a lot," Gabe observed drily.

"Hey, they were on me like a shot," Mick retorted. "I never had a chance to get a good look at them."

"And they said you'd better shut it down?" Gabe looked perplexed. "Shut *what* down?"

Mick shrugged. "I think they meant Fleet Street."

"But why?"

"Good question." Mick limped over to the corner where the coffeepot was located. He poured the remains of the pot into a chipped mug and took a sip. "Blech!" he choked. "This tastes like mud."

"It should," Gabe said with a grin. "It was made yesterday. I just reheated it."

Mick stared for a long moment at the thick sludge in his cup. "I just don't get it. Why would two guys in a fancy car want to put us out of business? Because they think we're too successful and they want to get rid of the competition?"

"Successful? That's a laugh," Gabe quipped. "I mean, we're drinking day-old coffee out of broken mugs." He rubbed his chin with his hand thoughtfully. "How do you know for sure it was you they were after? Did they call you by name?"

Mick looked up in confusion. "What do you mean?"

"It's like this." Gabe crossed his burly arms across his chest. "I'm co-owner of this outfit, and no one's roughed me up."

"Wait a minute!" Mick sat up so fast his head hurt. "What if they really did think I was someone else? Like my cousin Charlie."

"Mick, get real!" Gabe cried in exasperation.

"Well, people always say we look a lot alike," Mick replied. He narrowed his eyes. "And Charlie's working for Fleet Street now. It would be just like him to get mixed up in some kind of trouble."

"Aw, come on, man," Gabe said. "Charlie's only been with us a week."

"That's more than enough time for him to do serious damage to our business."

"But how?" Gabe asked, putting the supplies back in the first-aid kit.

"I don't know." Mick took another sip of coffee, this time not even noticing the bitter taste. "Maybe he's using Fleet Street as a front for something else." When Gabe gave him a disbelieving look, Mick slammed the cup down on the desk. "Or maybe someone else is!"

Gabe, who was sliding the white metal box into the bottom of one of the lockers, looked up in shock. "You mean, one of our riders?"

Mick shrugged. "If Charlie could do it, so could any one of them."

"But who?" Gabe ticked off the messengers' names on one hand. "Phil Wilayto's a little weird but he's a good guy. Tyrone's our hardest worker, and Terry Han and Cynthia have been with us since the beginning." He shook his head in disbelief. "I trust all those people."

"All I know is two hoods gave me until midnight Thursday to shut my business down," Mick said stubbornly. "That gives me three and a half days to find out who's behind this, and why."

"But you're just making a lot of wild assumptions," Gabe countered. "Face the facts. You got mugged. What happened to you happens to somebody every day in this city."

Mick clenched his jaw tightly. "Yeah, people get robbed and beat up, but they don't get threatened like that."

Gabe sank down in the overstuffed couch and sighed heavily. "Well, if you feel so strongly that one of our riders is doing something illegal, you ought to be up front about it. I mean, ask them if they know what's going down."

"Oh, right." Mick rolled his eyes. "And I'm sure they'd tell me if they were."

"So why don't you hire a spy?" Gabe shot back. "Cleverly disguised as a bike messenger?"

"Gabe, you're a genius!"

His friend looked up in dismay. "I was only kidding!"

Mick paced back and forth in front of the desk, planning his strategy out loud. "We'll get someone in here who's completely trustworthy. Hire them as a new rider taking over Terry's slot while he's on vacation. No one would question that. It's obvious we're shorthanded."

"It's official," Gabe declared. "You're out of your mind."

"Then when the riders go out to make deliveries," Mick went on, "our spy can follow them and report back anything strange or unusual to us."

"You're just chasing shadows," Gabe protested.

"Maybe," Mick replied. "And maybe not."

"You're really serious about doing this, aren't you?"

"Absolutely."

Gabe looked at Mick for a long time. Finally he shrugged. "Well, if we get another rider, at least we'll catch up with our backlog of orders. But I just see one small *problemo*."

Mick stopped pacing and looked at his friend. "What's that?"

"Where are you going to find someone totally trustworthy, who can ride a bike, and be ready to go to work for us tomorrow morning"—he snapped his fingers—"like that?"

A smile crept across Mick's lips, lighting up his entire face. "I know just the person."

Mick strutted over to the desk, tossed the receiver in the air, and dialed a familiar number. An image of a girl with long brown hair, green eyes flashing with indignation or humor, went through his mind.

"Mick, what're you doing?" Gabe asked suspiciously. "Who are you calling ?"

The phone rang twice, then a voice answered clearly, "Amanda Hart speaking."

"Yo, Mandy, this is Mick."

"I don't believe this," Gabe muttered under his breath.

Mick grinned as he leaned comfortably on the edge of the desk. "Are you doing anything special for the next few days? I need your help."

CHAPTER THREE

Early the next morning Amanda Hart stood framed in the doorway of her aunt and uncle's Victorian home, watching the street. She took a sip of the coffee she was holding and smiled as her best friend, Pepper Larson, pulled her yellow Mustang convertible up to the curb. Without looking up, Pepper gave the horn one loud blast.

Amanda laughed and called, "You must be still asleep. Want some coffee?"

"Please!" Pepper croaked as she turned to face her friend. Pepper's red hair stuck out in all directions and her brown eyes were bloodshot and puffy behind the wire-rimmed glasses that perched on her freckled nose. She'd obviously just gotten up.

Amanda dashed into the kitchen and poured Pepper a mug of steaming-hot coffee, then checked herself in the hall mirror. She was dressed in khaki tennis shorts, a pink and white pin-striped blouse with a khaki vest, and a pair of sunglasses.

"I hope this outfit is okay," she murmured to her reflection. "Mick didn't say anything about uniforms, or a dress code."

Carefully balancing the two cups of coffee, Amanda glided down the steps. "Good morning," she sang out as she held one of the cups toward her friend.

"What's good about it?" Pepper squinted one eye shut to look at Amanda. "The first day of spring break, and you get me up at the shriek of dawn." She took a long, deep sip of coffee and sighed gratefully.

"I'm sorry to do this to you, Pep," Amanda said as she slid into the passenger seat. "But I just couldn't get my scooter started." Amanda pointed to the white motorbike leaning against the side of the house. "I think it's out of gas."

Pepper slipped the Mustang in first gear and sped off down Chestnut Street toward downtown San Francisco. "Why you would want to spend your spring break working as a bicycle messenger is beyond me," she said grumpily. "I wish you'd change your mind and come skiing. We're leaving for Lake Tahoe this afternoon."

"I'd love to go with you." Amanda flipped her sunglasses up on her head and tossed her brown hair over her shoulder. "But Mick asked me to help him and I think I owe him one."

The fact that Mick had asked *her* for help was a novel experience. Usually it was the other way around. Amanda had a knack for uncovering mysteries and getting to the bottom of them. Unfortunately that tendency often landed her in hot water.

Amanda smiled at her friend. "I have to admit, the idea of working on another case is pretty exciting."

"*Case?*" Pepper repeated. "You sound like a full-fledged detective."

Amanda took a sip of her coffee. "I wish."

"What about your dreams of being an ace reporter?" Pepper asked.

"They're sort of the same thing, don't you think?" Amanda replied. "I mean, a reporter finds out who, what, where, and why. And so does a detective. A reporter just writes about it—"

"And becomes rich and famous," Pepper cut in. "Like your mom and dad."

Amanda's parents, Del and Dinah Hart, were world-renowned photojournalists. They'd twice won the Pulitzer Prize for their reporting on the Vietnam War and the conflict in Northern Ireland. Amanda dreamed of following in their footsteps. After only six months at Sutter Academy she had already become editor in chief of the school paper, the *Sutter Spectator*. Pepper was the staff photographer, which was how they had originally become friends.

"I heard from them yesterday," Amanda said,

taking a sip of her coffee. "They're in Nepal. Dad's sick, and Mom is sunburned."

"Serves them right for going there without you," Pepper cracked. Her voice softened as she added, "It must have been nice to hear from them."

Amanda smiled and nodded. Because her parents were constantly on the road, they had decided it was best for Amanda to stay in one place till she graduated from high school. That was why Amanda had come to live with her relatives in San Francisco. She loved her aunt Jane and her uncle Silas, but being so far away from her parents wasn't easy. She missed them a lot.

It only took Pepper twenty minutes to drive from the Marina to a narrow side street near the corner of Mission and Market streets. She pulled up to the curb in front of a tidy little corner grocery store. SANCHEZ GROCERY was painted in red lettering across the windows.

"It just occurred to me," Pepper said, putting her car in neutral. "If you're supposed to be a bicycle messenger, where's your bike?"

Amanda looped her purse over her shoulder and opened the door of the Mustang. "Mick said I could use Terry Han's while he's on vacation."

"That's a relief. I was going to offer you my old Schwinn but I think it's rusted to the bike rack in our garage."

"Thanks," Amanda said with a grin. "But these guys use special bikes for this business. I think I heard Mick mention something called a Rockhopper."

"Oh, yeah, that's one of those bikes with the thick tires," Pepper said. "It helps those crazy messengers ride even faster as they break all the traffic laws."

"I know what you mean." More than once Amanda had been forced to leap back onto the curb as a cyclist sped through a red light. "Well, I'm going to be a different kind of messenger. I'm going to obey the traffic rules, and go slow."

"You do that, and you'll stick out like a sore thumb," Pepper cautioned. "Aren't you supposed to be working undercover?"

"Right. Mick's promised to give me a crash course in this whole messenger business this morning."

"This is your last chance to forsake all of this nonsense and come skiing *avec moi,*" Pepper called as Amanda got out of the car.

"Thanks, Pepper, but—"

"I know, I know," Pepper said, rolling her eyes. "Mick needs you." Then she leaned across the seat and added, "Don't mind me, I'm just jealous. If I had a hunk like Mick Soul calling me, you can bet my skiing days would be history." She glanced at herself in the mirror and grimaced. "I'm going to go home and see what I can do about rearranging my face. Then I'm off in search of Mr. Wonderful on the slopes. Wish me luck!"

"Happy hunting!" Amanda called.

Pepper beeped the horn twice and then sped up the street. Amanda watched until the yellow Mustang had disappeared around the corner. Then she squared her shoulders and walked in quick strides past the grocery.

Amanda stepped into the alley behind the store and headed for the cement steps with the rusty bike rack chained to the banister. A figure dressed in a worn leather jacket and jeans was leaning casually against the brick wall, with one foot propped up behind him. He heard her footsteps and looked up.

Amanda's pulse instantly quickened as his deep blue eyes met hers. She knew Mick was handsome, but somehow she always forgot just *how* handsome he was until she saw him again.

"Mandy." A pleased smile spread across his lips. "Am I glad to see you!" The throaty rumble of his voice made her skin tingle.

As Mick moved to join her, she suddenly had second thoughts and whispered, "Look, Mick, I'm more than willing to help you, but I'm a little concerned about trying to be a messenger."

"It'll be a piece of cake," Mick replied confidently. "I'll give you a quick rundown on the whole procedure before you have to deliver anything."

Mick glanced over his shoulder, then pulled her to the side of the building and lowered his voice to an urgent whisper. "The important thing is to act like we've never met. I told the other riders that I hired you as a replacement for Terry while he's on vacation."

"But they're going to expect me to be a pro at this stuff," Amanda protested.

"A day or two on the bike and you'll *be* a pro."

A worried frown wrinkled her brow. "But what exactly am I looking for?"

"I'm not sure. But I want you to follow my riders, write down where they go, and when, and report back to me." He ran his hand through his hair. "I guess I'm looking for some break in the routine."

"That's a lot of work," Amanda said. "How much time do I have?"

"Three days."

"Three days?"

"Don't worry," Mick reassured her. "Gabe and I will be working with you. The three of us should be able to solve this thing in no time."

Amanda shook her head. "I wish I had your confidence."

"You'll be fine, believe me." Mick reached out and touched her cheek with his fingertips. "I really appreciate this. I owe you one, Mandy." He stared into her green eyes for a long moment. Then he pulled away abruptly. "Come on. I want you to meet the gang."

As he opened the door, Mick whispered, "Remember, keep your eyes and ears open for anything unusual—and you and I don't know each other."

"Right." Amanda swallowed hard and then stepped through the door into Fleet Street. She was immediately hit with the sound of loud music blaring from a radio somewhere.

"I told you, we're understaffed right now." A figure dressed in what looked like a surfer's wet-suit and a red warm-up jacket was yelling hoarsely into the telephone at the battered old desk. "So tell me when you need it, and we'll be there."

Off in the corner a thickly muscled fellow was repairing a yellow ten-speed propped up on a bench. In his black T-shirt, jeans, and red bandanna, the guy looked as tough as nails. But Amanda knew better.

"Gabe!" she murmured happily.

At the sound of his name, Gabe turned and burst into a huge grin. He opened his mouth to greet her but Mick hurriedly cut in. "This is our new rider, Amanda Hart."

Mick shot his partner a warning glance and Gabe's face became impassive. He nodded shortly and said, "Nice to meet you."

"Listen up, you guys," Mick shouted. "I've got an announcement to make."

The person at the desk hung up the phone and spun to face the group. With a start Amanda realised that *he* was a *she*. Her hair was pulled up under her cap and she stood with her feet spread apart, like a jock.

Mick never mentioned he had a girl *working for*

him, Amanda thought to herself. *Especially a* pretty *girl.*

"So who's this?" the girl said, gesturing to Amanda.

"This is Amanda Hart," Mick replied. "She's filling in for Terry Han while he's on vacation."

The girl coolly looked Amanda up and down. "*You're* a bike messenger?" From the tone of her voice it was obvious she didn't think so.

Before Amanda could reply, a goofy-looking guy in baggy pants and a Hawaiian shirt stepped forward and put out his hand. "Phil Wilayto. Welcome aboard."

"Hi, Phil," Amanda said. She turned back to the girl and said stiffly, "I didn't catch your name."

"That's became I didn't say it," the girl said with a thin smile. "Cynthia Spartaro."

"Nice to meet—"

"Mick, did you get these dispatches here?" Cynthia cut Amanda off and scooped up a handful of yellow slips from the desk. "The phone's been going crazy all morning."

"So let's quit talkin', and get ridin'," Mick replied. "Where's Tyrone?"

"Still out," Gabe rumbled. "We've got to double up again."

"Right." Mick sat down at the desk and quickly sorted the dispatches into groups. The phone rang again, and without looking up Mick said, "Get that, would you, Cyn?"

Cynthia sat on the desk next to Mick and picked up the phone. "Fleet Street." She asked a few questions as she filled out a blank yellow form from a pile sitting next to her. After she hung up, Cynthia held up the new dispatch. "Higgins, Bloom and Blackstock, across from the Montgomery Street BART station. Any takers?"

Phil reached for the dispatch but Mick said, "I think this would be a good one for Amanda to take."

Amanda looked stunned. "But . . ."

"I could explain to you how we work here at Fleet Street," Mick continued, "but I think it's best for you to just dive in."

Amanda's eyes widened. She had no idea what to do.

Mick saw her panicked look and said reassuringly, "Hey, it's okay. I'm sending my most experienced rider along to break you in."

Amanda breathed a sigh of relief. She turned to smile at Phil when Mick said, "Cynthia knows the whole procedure cold. If there's something she doesn't know about the messenger service, then it's not worth knowing."

Cynthia leaned over and put her face close to Mick's. "If I'm so valuable," she purred, "how come I haven't gotten a raise?"

"When the money comes gushing in," Mick replied with a chuckle, "you'll be the first in the receiving line. In the meantime, you'll just have to accept my undying gratitude."

Cynthia hopped off the desk. "That and fifty cents will buy me a cup of coffee."

Amanda watched the two of them tease each

other and fought back the wave of jealousy that was growing inside her. Mick and Cynthia seemed so comfortable together, like brother and sister, or maybe a couple who'd been going together for years. On top of it, Mick was acting as if she didn't even exist.

I don't need this, Amanda thought angrily. *I should just go skiing with Pepper and let Mick handle his little problems himself. That would show him a thing or two.*

"Hello. Anybody home?"

Amanda jerked back into focus. Cynthia stood in front of her, strapping a bike helmet onto her head. "I was saying, where's your bike?"

"Bike?"

Cynthia rolled her eyes. "This *is* a bicycle messenger service. You *are* a bicycle messenger. You *will* need a bike." She spoke the words with exaggerated slowness, as if she were talking to a six-year-old. "Or didn't that occur to you?"

"I'm well aware of that," Amanda snapped. "It's just that Mick—that is your name, isn't it?" She glared at him hard. "He said something about letting me use Terry Han's."

Cynthia pointed to the yellow ten-speed Gabe had been working on that was now hanging from a hook in the ceiling. "That's it over there."

Amanda hesitated, unsure of how to get the bike down.

"And step on it, will you?" Cynthia added. "We're called Fleet Street, not Slow Joe's."

The boys burst out laughing, but Amanda narrowed her eyes angrily and hurried over to the bike. She didn't find Cynthia's crack the least bit amusing. Mick leaped up from the desk and moved quickly to help her.

"You're doing great," he whispered as he swung the bike onto the floor.

Amanda shot him a dirty look and hissed, "No thanks to you!"

Mick grinned. "Don't let Cynthia's attitude get to you. She's tough as nails on the outside, but inside—she's a real marshmallow. You'll hit it off great." Before Amanda could reply, he slapped her on the back and declared, "Now, go on, get outta here!"

Amanda wheeled the bike out the door and bounced it down the steps to the alley. Cynthia was already there, pointedly tapping her fingers on her handlebars. Amanda barely had time to slip her feet into the bike stirrups before Cynthia peeled out in a spray of gravel.

"Hey!" Amanda shouted. "Wait for me!"

CHAPTER FOUR

For Amanda, the next fifteen minutes were straight out of a nightmare. Cynthia only rode her bike one way—at breakneck speed. She was also oblivious to any of the usual rules of the road. Cynthia had a police whistle on a cord around her neck and at every crosswalk would blow it loudly, then speed on through. More than once she missed colliding with a startled pedestrian by mere inches.

The minute Amanda caught up, Cynthia would sprint away and weave in and out of traffic. It was as if she were daring Amanda to try and stick with her.

"She's out to prove I can't cut this," Amanda muttered under her breath. "Well, we'll see about that." She dug down into her last reserve of strength and gamely pursued the other cyclist. From that moment on, no matter what Cynthia did, Amanda stuck to her like glue.

First Cynthia pushed the yellow light at the intersection, forcing Amanda to run the red light to keep from losing her. Then she tried to break Amanda's endurance by going up a few murderous hills. The last straw came as Cynthia veered onto a one-way street and drove right down the center line between the oncoming rows of cars.

"No way," Amanda declared. "I'm not committing suicide." She pulled over to the curb and popped up onto the sidewalk. Luckily the pavement was uncrowded. Amanda struggled to keep Cynthia in sight while she steered clear of the fireplugs and mailboxes that loomed up in her path.

By the time Amanda reached her, Cynthia had looped her bike lock around a parking meter and removed the front wheel of her bike by the sprockets. Carrying it easily in one hand, she loped up the steps of a gray marble office building.

When Amanda slid off the bike onto the pavement, her legs suddenly felt wobbly. Amanda grabbed the parking meter and held on for dear life. After a second she found she could stand again. She unwrapped the bicycle chainlock from around the seat and realized that she didn't know the combination. Finally she just leaned her bike against Cynthia's, looped the chain around the meter, and hoped for the best. Then she hurried into the office building.

"What took you so long?" Cynthia demanded as Amanda joined her at the reception desk. A woman behind the counter was in the process of initialing the little yellow form Amanda recognized as the dispatching slip from Fleet Street.

Amanda forced a smile as she bent over to catch her breath. "I guess I'm just a little out of shape."

"Here you go." The office worker handed Cynthia a manila envelope with an address printed on the outside. Cynthia checked it with a quick glance and nodded. "Not far—just down Battery this side of Broadway. Come on."

Cynthia was back out on the sidewalk before Amanda had a chance to react. By the time Amanda caught up with her, she was already straddling her bike, preparing to shove off into traffic.

"Look," Amanda said, grabbing Cynthia's handlebars, "you've shown me how fast you are, and I'm impressed. But Mick said you would also show me the ropes. So why don't you start by explaining a few things."

Cynthia stared at her mutely.

"For instance, who pays?" Amanda continued. "Do clients sign for their deliveries, do they have a running account back at Fleet Street—or is it cash only? That sort of thing."

Cynthia leaned back and squinted one eye at Amanda. "How did Mick ever find you?"

"I, uh, contacted him," Amanda replied. "And he just happened to have a temporary opening."

"But you've never done this before, have you?"

"What makes you say that?" Amanda countered defensively.

"That outfit, for one thing." Cynthia waved a hand at Amanda's trim appearance. "I mean, come on! You look like you're off for an afternoon of tennis at the club."

"Well, where I come from," Amanda sputtered, "messengers dress like this."

Cynthia rested one hand on her hip. "And where *do* you come from?"

Amanda's mind raced for a quick reply. Then she spotted a poster of a white beach and tropical palms in the window of a travel agency across the street and blurted, "Bermuda."

"Bermuda!" Cynthia almost looked impressed.

"Yes. You see, there are very few cars on the island, and practically everyone rides a bike or a moped."

"Really?"

"Oh, yes. But we never have to deal with the kind of traffic you have here in San Francisco or the hills." Amanda knelt beside Terry's bike as she spoke, and keeping her back to Cynthia, she acted as if she were unlocking the bike. She made a show of looping the chain around her neck as she had seen some other cyclists do. "So on our way to this next delivery," Amanda continued casually, "why don't you give me the lowdown on how things are done in an American messenger service?"

Cynthia shrugged and slipped back out into traffic. "The basic procedure goes like this," Cynthia called over her shoulder as they sped along. "You pick up the package or envelope from an office rep and have them authorize delivery. Don't under any circumstances *ever* peek inside—that's like a federal offense. And then you deliver it to the address. Oh, yeah, get a signature when you drop it off. That's all there is to it."

"So who pays for it?"

"If they have an account, it'll say so on the order slip or they'll fill in the authorized number. Otherwise, they pay on the spot. Better check every time, too, unless they're a regular." Cynthia motioned with her head for Amanda to pull over. "There it is—Ridley, Stein and Carpenter."

They glided up in front of the Battery Street law office and Amanda smoothly leaped off her bike. To her surprise, Cynthia pulled the manila envelope out of her bag and tossed it to Amanda. "You make the delivery. I'll wait out here."

"Right. Hold my bike." Amanda turned and ran briskly up the steps into the old brick building.

Once she was inside the reception area, Amanda leaned gratefully against the wall and rubbed her aching calves. "My first trip out, and already my legs feel like limp spaghetti," she muttered under her breath. There was a big smear of grease on her sock from the bike chain. With a sigh, Amanda forced herself to straighten up and march into the office.

The delivery was simple. The secretary signed for the letter and Amanda slipped the receipt into her bag. Then she hurried back out to where Cynthia was waiting. To Amanda's frustration the other girl didn't even ask how it went but announced, "I called Fleet Street. We've got a couple more stops to make. So let's move it!"

Once again Cynthia was off like a shot. "What is this," Amanda shouted, "a race?" Her voice was lost in the raucous blare of traffic.

Cynthia led them down a side street up to the door of a tiny storefront. A faded sign hung above the entrance.

"J and L Office Supply," Amanda read out loud.

"Yeah, what a dump, huh?" Cynthia said, pulling a stack of papers out of her bag. "I'll be right back."

Amanda waved limply. "Take your time. I'm not going anywhere."

Cynthia pulled open the door to the store and a bell rang as she stepped inside. The door shut with a swooshing sound and Amanda slumped over her handlebars.

The side street was cool and quiet after the hubbub of the city traffic. High above her head Amanda could glimpse a thin blue line of sky between the tops of the buildings, dappled with white clouds. She turned her head and peered inside the office supply shop.

Cynthia was standing at a messy counter cluttered with boxes of ballpoint pens, rolls of plastic tape, and packets of envelopes. A heavy man emerged from the rear of the store and Cynthia shoved the stack of papers in his direction. He picked them up and nodded. Then the messenger turned and headed for the door.

Amanda jerked upright, hoping Cynthia hadn't noticed her looking so tired. "Where to now?" she shouted as Cynthia hopped onto her bike.

"The TransAmerica building."

Amanda nodded and followed Cynthia to the San Francisco landmark. It was shaped like a big, skinny pyramid and was located on the edge of the financial district.

As the two girls rounded the corner at Washington onto Montgomery Street, they nearly collided with another cyclist. It was Mick.

"I thought I'd come join you on your first day of work," he said as they pulled their bikes up onto the sidewalk to talk. He glanced from one girl to the other and nodded approvingly. "You seem to have it under control. How are things going?"

Amanda wanted to shout "Terrible!" at the top of her lungs, but she wasn't about to let Cynthia know she was having a hard time. Instead she said with a tight smile, "Things are just fine."

"Yeah, the day's half over and we've only made two stops," Cynthia remarked sarcastically. "Just fine." Cynthia checked her watch and whistled between her teeth. "Hey, if I don't deliver this soon, those brokers will wish they'd used the post office."

"Look, Cyn," Mick said suddenly, "you go on alone. I want to take Amanda back to Fleet Street—"

"For some private coaching?" Cynthia cut in with a knowing look.

Mick raised an eyebrow, then nodded. "Yeah. You might say that."

"I see."

Amanda blushed, but turned and said, "Thanks for the—"

But Cynthia was on her bike and gone before Amanda could finish the sentence. She turned back to Mick and said sourly, "Nice girl."

"Aw, don't mind Cyn," Mick replied. "Like I told you before—she's tough as nails on the outside but a real marshmallow at heart."

"Oh? Well, I still don't believe it." Amanda felt a sudden pang of jealousy as she recalled how intimate Mick had seemed with Cynthia back at Fleet Street.

"Come on, you need a break." Mick took her bicycle by the handlebars and started to push both bikes down the sidewalk. "I'll buy you a Coke."

Amanda smiled with relief. "I could use a cool drink right now. Thanks."

They crossed the street toward the diner on the corner. As they reached the curb, Mick stopped in his tracks. "Oh, no," he groaned. "Not him."

Amanda looked in the direction Mick was staring and gasped with surprise. Lounging on one of the worn red leather stools was a boy who could have easily passed for Mick's twin brother.

CHAPTER FIVE

"Mickey! What a surprise!" The other boy rose to his feet and gestured to the empty chair beside him. "Take a load off."

Amanda stared openmouthed at the two boys. They were exactly the same height, just under six feet tall, with the same lock of dark hair falling lazily over the forehead. Each had the same strong chin, softened by a small cleft dividing it. But they had radically different styles of dressing. Mick wore faded jeans, a white T-shirt, and a worn leather jacket, whereas the other boy was fashionably clad in baggy pleated khakis and an oversize red-and-yellow sweater. A pair of dark sunglasses dangled from a cord around his neck.

"I can't believe you, Charlie," Mick snapped.

"One week on the job and you're hanging out in cafés."

"Now, hold it," Charlie protested, stubbing out the cigarette he'd been smoking. "I was just taking a little break."

"After one delivery you need a break?"

"Look, I just ordered a cup of coffee, then I was going to be on my way. Really."

"Right." Mick looked unconvinced. "I want to see your logbook at the end of the day. I gave you a job, not a paid vacation."

"Mickey." Charlie assumed a hurt look. "Is that any way to speak to your own flesh and blood?"

"I knew it!" Amanda blurted suddenly. "What are you two, brothers?"

"Cousins," Mick replied without a trace of a smile. "Unfortunately."

Charlie's face brightened at the sight of Amanda. "I didn't realize we had company. Introduce me."

"Amanda Hart." Mick gestured impatiently at his cousin. "Charlie Driscoll. He's *supposed* to be one of my riders."

"So am I." Amanda smiled and shook Charlie's hand. "But so far I'm having a rocky first day."

"You work for Fleet Street?" The boy fixed his dark blue eyes on her and grinned. "This job is getting better by the minute."

Amanda noticed out of the corner of her eye that Mick was watching her closely. Inexplicably that made her feel like flirting. She tossed her head and laughed.

Mick checked his watch and then cleared his throat. "If you're not back on the street in sixty seconds, Charlie, I'm going to find a new messenger."

His cousin signaled the waitress for his check. "Don't mind Mick," Charlie whispered conspiratorially in Amanda's ear. "He's tough as nails on the outside, but inside—"

"He's a real marshmallow," Amanda finished for him.

Charlie cocked his head and grinned. "Hey, you're all right, Mandy."

They not only look alike, Amanda thought to herself as she watched Charlie pay the waitress, *they talk alike.*

"Mandy, it was a pleasure meeting you." Charlie slipped his sunglasses on his nose and then turned to Mick. "See you back at the ranch."

As Charlie coasted away from the curb, Mick grumbled, half to himself, "I just don't like that guy."

"Obviously," Amanda said drily.

Mick looked at her in surprise. Then, for the first time in ten minutes, he smiled. "You probably think I'm a jerk."

"No. I just wonder why you dislike Charlie when you two seem to be so much alike."

"*Seem.*" Mick raised his forefinger in the air. "That's the important word in that sentence."

The waitress arrived and Mick ordered a couple of colas. Then he leaned their bikes up against the wall where he could watch them and sat down beside Amanda.

"When we were growing up, people always used to mistake us for twins. We were as close as brothers—for a while." Mick shook his head roughly. "But that's been over for a long time." A hard edge returned to his voice. "Charlie Driscoll's always spelled trouble for me, with a capital *T*."

"If you feel that strongly about him," Amanda asked, "why'd you give him a job?"

Mick looked up ruefully. "I've been asking myself the same question." He shrugged his shoulders. "The answer is, he needed a job and we were shorthanded. And he swore he'd behave."

"Behave?"

"On the surface, I know Charlie seems like a lot of fun but . . . basically he's a liar and a thief."

The waitress brought their drinks and Mick paid her. Amanda took a long sip from her cup. "I don't know about Charlie being a thief," she said thoughtfully, "but he certainly does stretch the truth."

Mick arched an eyebrow. "What do you mean?"

"Charlie said he'd just gotten here, but look." Amanda pointed to the overflowing metal ashtray. "This is full and they're all his brand. And these prove that he had more than one cup of coffee." She gestured toward the torn packs of sugar and empty cream cartons littered beside Charlie's empty coffee cup. "He was sitting here a long time. Which means he wasn't telling you the truth."

Mick shook his head in amazement. "You're good, you know that?"

Amanda shrugged modestly. "It's just simple observation, that's all."

"So . . ." Mick thought out loud. "This means Charlie might have been waiting to meet someone."

A sudden honking of horns turned their attention back to the street. A cyclist in a red jogging suit with white stripes down the sleeves and pants wove in and out of the swiftly moving traffic. He held a whistle in his mouth that he blew loudly as he ran the red light.

"Tyrone!" Mick nearly choked on his drink. He slammed his cup down on the table and in one move was on his bike, pedaling off into traffic. "Follow me!"

A startled Amanda tossed their cups in the trash and fumbled to get on her bike. Off in the distance she could see Mick threading his way through taxicabs and delivery trucks. He turned right abruptly and disappeared around the corner.

"All right, Mr. Soul," she announced out loud. "I'll follow you—but if you're not in plain sight when I turn that corner, I'm heading home, phoning Pepper, and going skiing."

Mick had stopped halfway up the block. He was standing on the sidewalk, talking intently with the rider who'd whizzed past them at the corner café.

Both boys had dismounted, leaving their bikes near the curb.

As Amanda coasted up beside them, she quickly sized up the black rider Mick had called Tyrone. He was lean, and a full head taller than Mick. A pair of gold wire-rimmed glasses sat on his nose, which gave him a slightly bookish look.

"Tyrone Waters," Mick announced as Amanda joined them. "Meet Amanda Hart, Fleet Street's newest recruit."

Tyrone limped across the sidewalk, favoring his left ankle, and extended his hand. "Welcome."

"Thanks." Amanda shook his hand and noticed that his grip was firm, but gentle. She gestured to his leg and asked, "Did you hurt your foot?"

Tyrone nodded. "I sprained it three days ago. I was just telling Mick here, I thought I'd try to exercise it a little today." Tyrone bent down and gingerly poked his ankle. "But it's still pretty sore."

"Ty's been having a rough winter," Mick explained. "He's caught every cold and flu that came through town."

Amanda suppressed a look of surprise. Tyrone looked like one of the healthiest people she'd ever seen. His clear brown eyes sparkled with energy. *Definitely not the type to give in to a common cold,* Amanda thought.

"I hope you'll be back with us tomorrow," Mick added, clapping Tyrone lightly on the shoulder. "We really need you."

"You can count on me, brother." Tyrone gave Mick a low five. As he limped back to his bike, he called over his shoulder to Amanda, "I'm looking forward to working with you, Amanda."

"Same here," she replied.

Tyrone straddled his bike and spun the front wheel. The bicycle turned in a circle and Tyrone raised his hand in mock salute. "Hi ho, Silver, away!" he called with a laugh. Then he straightened the front wheel and was gone like a shot.

"Quite impressive," Amanda declared.

Mick nodded as he retrieved his bike. "Yeah, Tyrone's a real trick cyclist."

"He's also a trick walker," she murmured under her breath.

Mick glanced over at her. "What do you mean?"

"His sprained ankle switched from his left to his right while we were talking."

"You noticed that, too?"

Mick looped his arm through Amanda's. "Come on. Let's get back to Fleet Street. Some very weird things are going down."

The way back was mostly downhill, for which Amanda was grateful. Soon the familiar facade of the Sanchez grocery came into view. As they entered the narrow alley in back of the grocery, Mick grabbed the seat of his bike and leaped off. Amanda did the same, proud of how well she executed the maneuver.

Suddenly a black sedan turned into the far end of the alley and Mick instantly dropped his bike.

"That's them," he hissed. "The guys who jumped me."

Mick leaped into a small recess of the building directly across the alley from Fleet Street. Amanda, still holding her bike, stood frozen in the middle of the alley as the menacing car drove slowly toward her.

"I don't think they saw me," Mick called from his hiding place.

"But they will," Amanda said, staring wide-eyed at the black sedan. "That car is going to be here any second. What should I do?"

"First of all, stop looking scared," Mick directed. "Smile."

Amanda plastered a phony smile across her face. "Now what?"

"Now look at me and laugh."

Amanda turned her head swiftly toward Mick and forced out a small chuckle.

"No good," Mick barked. "Really laugh. Throw your head back."

Amanda did as she was told and a high-pitched shriek came out of her mouth. But it must have convinced the men in the car because one leaned out of his side window and shouted at her, "Hey, honey, what's so funny?"

The car was getting closer and Amanda choked out in her best flirty voice, "Wouldn't you like to know?"

"Good," Mick whispered. Then to her surprise

he reached out his hand and pulled her into the shadows with him. "Now kiss me."

She obeyed without thinking, pressing her lips to his as his arms tightened around her back.

With his lips still against hers, Mick whispered, "I don't want them to see my face. So act like you're enjoying this."

Mick ran his hand under her hair and gently massaged her neck. Amanda felt a jolt of electricity that went all the way down to her toes. She didn't need to act—she was enjoying every minute of it.

As the car rolled slowly by them, Amanda tried to keep her mind clear and remember that this was all just an act, that a very real danger lurked right behind them.

"Hey, dude!" one of the men shouted as the car passed them. "Give her a kiss for me!"

Amanda could feel Mick's heart pounding against hers. They held the position for what seemed like an eternity, listening intently.

Suddenly the black car accelerated and with a squeal of tires spun out of the alley into the street.

Amanda's knees instantly went weak. She didn't know if it was from the kiss, or fear. But she barely had time to recover when Mick pulled away.

He grabbed her hand and barked, "Come on, let's get inside." Mick paused long enough to slip their bikes into the rack and lock them, then hurried up the steps to the door. "We'll be safe now."

Mick put his hand on the doorknob and Amanda felt her stomach tighten. On the other side of the door angry voices were shouting at each other.

CHAPTER SIX

"What do you mean, it's not fair?" Gabe was shouting as Mick and Amanda stepped into Fleet Street. "I've already advanced you two weeks' salary. Now let's drop it, okay?"

Phil Wilayto was standing nose-to-nose with Gabe. The slightly built rider seemed frail beside Gabe's massive physique but he held his ground. "I thought we were friends, but I guess I was wrong."

"This has nothing to do with friendship," Gabe replied ever.ly. "I told you the situation. I'm not a bank, Phil."

"Okay, be that way!" Phil exploded angrily, throwing his hands up in frustration. "If I can't get it here, I'll get the money somewhere else."

He rammed his beanie on his head, slung his

bag over his shoulder, and snapped, "Who needs you, anyway?"

Mick and Amanda flattened themselves on either side of the doorsill as Phil stomped out of the building.

"What's got into him?" Mick asked, stepping into the room.

Gabe scratched his head. "I don't know. Phil's the last guy I would have expected to be so weird about money."

"He's got quite a temper," Amanda said, moving toward the locker Mick had assigned her.

"I've never seen it before." Mick tossed his pack on the couch. "Usually Phil's really easygoing."

"Yeah, he's always cracking jokes," Gabe added. "Bad jokes."

"I just hope we haven't lost another rider," Mick said. "We need everyone we can get."

"Aw, Phil's just mouthing off." Gabe put the logbooks back into the desk drawer and straightened up. "He'll be back tomorrow, making the same dumb jokes."

"What's going on around here, anyway?" Mick grumbled. "Everyone's acting weird."

"What do you mean?" Gabe asked, slipping on his black denim jacket.

"Amanda and I saw Tyrone down in the financial district," Mick explained.

"So?"

"So he's been out for three days with a sprained ankle. Yet this morning I see him riding like a maniac downtown. And his so-called sprain doesn't seem to be bothering him at all."

"Maybe he just needed to take some time off," Gabe murmured as he locked the cashbox and tucked it under his arm.

"So why hide it from us? We're pretty tight with our people. What's he trying to pull?"

"I don't know, man." Gabe checked his watch. "Listen, Mick, I've got to run. I know it's my turn to close up, but will you do it tonight?"

"Sure, but—"

Gabe patted the cashbox under his arm. "I'll lock this away in my dad's safe."

"But I really think we need to talk," Mick insisted. "Those guys in the limo were back. Mandy and I just saw them outside—"

Gabe cut him off. "First thing tomorrow, I promise." Gabe was out of the room and had shut the door before Mick had a chance to protest.

Amanda listened to their exchange in bewilderment. If Gabe was really worried about Fleet Street and Mick's safety, he would have stayed to talk. Instead, he couldn't get out of there fast enough.

Hardly a minute had passed before the door swung open again, nearly hitting Amanda in the face. An irate Cynthia Spartaro marched right up to Mick and slammed her pack down on the desk.

"What's the idea of sticking me with that bimbo?" she snapped. "She can hardly ride a bike and she's dressed like a preppy Girl Scout. What's going on here?"

"It's simple," Mick growled impatiently. "Terry's out of town, Tyrone is pushing the limits of sick leave, and I am shorthanded. Besides, I can hire anyone I want."

"Yeah?" Cynthia snorted. "Just remember, I'm a cyclist, not a baby-sitter."

Mick slammed his hand down on the desk with a bang. "And just remember, I'm the boss."

Amanda felt totally humiliated. It took every ounce of her courage to step out from behind the cardboard boxes and clear her throat. "Uh, Mick," she called as she strode across the room to her lockers, "I'll be going home now."

Cynthia's jaw fell open and even Mick looked as if he'd forgotten Amanda was there. Amanda didn't give either one of them time to speak. She threw open her locker and looped her purse over her shoulder. "If you still need me tomorrow, give me a call, because I have better ways to use my time."

Then she forced herself to look at Cynthia as she added, "And from now on, I ride solo—or I don't ride at all." Amanda flipped her hair over her shoulder and walked coolly out the door.

Once she was standing in the alley, Amanda turned and faced the door with her hands on her hips.

"I may not be the best cyclist," Amanda grumbled under her breath. "And I may not be the most experienced messenger. And I may be a little out of shape." Her voice rose to an indignant howl. "But I am *not* a bimbo!"

She aimed a kick at the side of the green dumpster and the muscle in her calf immediately knotted up. Amanda hurriedly massaged it and then hobbled down the alley toward the bus stop.

When she got home, Amanda grabbed an apple from the refrigerator and then limped up the stairs to her bedroom. Every muscle in her body ached. All she could think about was taking a hot bath and going straight to bed. As she walked into the room, she was greeted by the ring of her phone.

"That's Mick," she thought, hurrying over to the bedside table. "He's calling to apologize." Amanda dropped her pack to the floor, sat on the edge of the bed, and sank gratefully back onto the fluffy pillows of her big brass bed. "And it's about time, too."

She picked up the receiver, but before she could say hello, a familiar voice said, "It's me."

"Pepper?" Amanda struggled to sit up. "What happened? You're supposed to be in Lake Tahoe."

"Yeah," Pepper said dully. "Hot dogging my way down the slopes. It's hard to do that when there's no snow. And it's not even cold enough for the snow machines."

"What?" Amanda straightened her back.

"Apparently whoever scheduled our spring break forgot to inform the weatherman that I was going skiing."

"What are you going to do?"

"It's too late to join the Spanish Club's trip to Mexico," Pepper cracked. "They left this morning. Mom and Dad suggested we wait a few days."

"Wait for what?" Amanda asked, taking a loud bite out of her apple. "A blizzard?"

"I'd settle for six inches of light, fluffy powder. The weatherman says the temperature's going to drop this evening. So . . ." Pepper took a long pause. "That gives you a chance to change your mind, and join me."

"Oh, Pepper. I'd love to." Amanda arched her back, feeling the knots of soreness between her shoulder blades. "There isn't a part of my body that doesn't hurt. But—"

"I know, I know," Pepper cut in. "Mick needs you."

"That's what he said yesterday," Amanda said. "But after today, I'm not so sure I'm the one who can help him."

"Well, did you notice anything suspicious going on?"

"Everything," Amanda replied. "We caught one rider—Tyrone—who called in sick today riding through the financial district like it was the Tour de France. And another guy named Phil, who on the surface seems kooky and kind of funny, got into a huge fight with Gabe about wanting money. He stormed out of there like he was going to go rob a bank."

"Is that all the riders Mick has?" Pepper asked. "That's not many. What about Terry Han?"

"He's on vacation; I'm taking his place." Amanda took another bite of her apple. There's also his cousin Charlie, who could pass for Mick's twin. He's awfully cute but Mick doesn't trust him at all."

"Do you think Mick's right?" Pepper interrupted.

"I can't say I blame him. We caught Charlie in an out-and-out lie this afternoon. He'd been at a café for quite a long time but he told us he'd only been there a few minutes." Amanda furrowed her brow. "And then there's Cynthia."

"A girl?"

"Yeah." Amanda bit angrily into the core of her apple.

"Oh." Pepper chuckled. "A cute girl."

"She's perfect," Amanda admitted. "Ultracool, a whiz on a bike, petite figure, with thick dark hair, very pretty, and"—she tossed the apple core into the trash can beside her bed—"I hate her."

"Do I detect a note of jealousy in Miss Amanda Hart's voice?"

"Maybe just a little," Amanda conceded. "Mixed with genuine dislike. Cynthia was a jerk to me all day. Which is why I can't quit. She'll think I'm a total wimp."

"So do you have any idea of what's going on at Fleet Street?"

"Not a clue. Everybody's acting weird, but it's going to take more time to figure it out." Her calf muscle contracted in another cramp and she moaned in pain. "Another day on that bike, and I won't be capable of walking, much less investigating."

"I've got an idea," Pepper announced.

Amanda listened, but there was nothing but silence on the line. "Well," she urged, "what is it?"

"Don't rush me," Pepper replied. "I'm thinking."

Amanda lay back on her pillow, waiting for Pepper to continue.

Finally Pepper said, "I've got to think some more about this. But unless there's a foot of snow in the Sierras tonight, I'll see you tomorrow morning at your house."

Before Amanda could reply there was a click and a dial tone on the line. Amanda chuckled as she returned the phone to its cradle. Pepper never said hello or good-bye when she called.

Amanda laid her head back on her pillow and stared at the ceiling. She ran over the events of the day one more time. Her thoughts kept returning to Cynthia. Something she had said earlier had struck a false chord, but Amanda couldn't remember what it was. She took a deep breath and closed her eyes, forcing herself to release the tension in her aching muscles.

Suddenly her eyes opened wide. When they had run into Mick on the street, Cynthia had said that they had made two stops together. But Amanda remembered they had actually made three. Was that a deliberate exclusion, or just an oversight? Amanda felt her eyelids grow heavy with sleep.

"Whatever it means," she thought drowsily, "it can wait until tomorrow."

CHAPTER SEVEN

The next morning Amanda stood in front of Mick's desk. She wore black tight-fitting cycle shorts that she'd borrowed from her friend Bonnie at school, a red tank top with a loose sweatshirt layered over it, and sleek black training shoes. She'd pulled her hair into a ponytail at the base of her neck and set a black wool tam on her head.

Mick leaned back in his desk chair, his hands looped behind his head. "I like it," he said, nodding approvingly. "Now you really look like one of us."

Amanda folded her arms across her chest. "A few wardrobe suggestions would have been appreciated yesterday. Being called a bimbo by Cynthia Spartaro is not my idea of a good time."

Mick took his feet off the desk and leaned forward. "Listen, I'm sorry about that. Cyn's usually really friendly. All of the guys get along with her great."

"I'll bet they do," Amanda said wryly. "Being the only girl at Fleet Street must be nice."

Mick chuckled. "Cynthia's probably just protecting her turf. Give her a little time. She'll warm up and you'll find out she's the best."

"I wanted to talk to you about that." Amanda pulled up one of the folding chairs that were stacked against the far wall and opened it. "There's something Cynthia said yesterday that's been bothering me." She held up her hand as Mick started to speak. "Besides calling me a bimbo."

Mick nodded attentively. "Fire away."

"Yesterday she told you we'd made two stops," Amanda explained. "When we'd actually made three."

Mick shrugged. "So?"

"So, either she forgot, or she was deliberately lying to hide something."

"That's an easy mistake for any rider to make," Mick said. "On a busy day they could make twenty to thirty stops. I can't expect them to remember the exact number."

"You said for me to watch for anything unusual," Amanda said with a shrug. "To my mind, saying we made two stops instead of three is unusual."

Mick studied her face closely and grinned his lopsided smile. "Are you sure you just don't have it in for Cyn?" he asked. "Since she gave you such a hard time?"

"What do you mean?"

"Maybe you're just a little jealous of my friendship with her."

"Jealous?" Amanda stood up so fast the folding chair fell back onto the floor with a clang. "Me?"

Mick chuckled and that made Amanda furious. She wanted to punch him in the nose. Here she was, sacrificing her spring break, and risking her life on a rickety bicycle, and he had the nerve to accuse her of being jealous. Amanda stared at him, quivering with anger.

Maybe she was jealous—just a little. But Cynthia Spartaro was still a possible suspect and Amanda wasn't about to forget it. She marched over to her locker just as Fleet Street exploded to life.

"Good morning, San Francisco!" Phil Wilayto said as he burst into the room. He was dressed in purple parachute pants, black-and-white-checked high-tops, and a silver warmup jacket, with a grin stretching from ear to ear. Amanda couldn't believe it was the same guy she'd seen get so angry the day before.

Tyrone, who was right behind Phil, covered his eyes in mock pain. "What are you trying to do, blind me? That outfit's too much to bear this early in the A.M."

"I'm dressing for success," Phil shot back.

"Success as what," Cynthia retorted as she entered the office, "a circus clown?"

Gabe appeared through the curtain that led to his father's grocery, carrying a pot of hot coffee and an open box of donuts. The riders swarmed around him as he put the food on the counter table.

"How's the foot, Tyrone?" Gabe asked, pouring himself some coffee.

Tyrone rubbed his right ankle. "One hundred and ten percent. That rest did me good." He clapped his hands and added, "I'm ready to get mobile and ride."

Cynthia stepped up to her locker and paused just long enough to take in Amanda's new look. "What'd you do, quit the Girl Scouts?"

"Yo, Cyn," Mick called from the desk. "Give Mandy a break."

"I was only joking," Cynthia said with a thin smile at Amanda. "I have to hand it to you, you learn fast."

The wall clock struck nine and the phone instantly started ringing.

"All right, boys and girls," Mick shouted as he reached for the receiver. "It's showtime!"

Within minutes he had assigned each rider their first round of deliveries.

"Mandy!" Mick hurriedly scribbled an address on a yellow piece of paper. "Embarcadero Center, two of them, go!" He thrust the paper in her hands and she ran with the other riders to their bikes outside.

Amanda hopped on the yellow ten-speed and pressed down hard into the pedals. She hoped Cynthia noticed that she was the first one out of the alley. Amanda put her head down and made a big show of pedaling as fast as she could down the street.

"Go, Amanda!" Tyrone and Phil cheered from behind her.

Amanda raised her hand in salute, took the next corner at breakneck speed, and collapsed behind a tin shed at the end of the block.

After taking a few moments to catch her breath, Amanda peered out of her hiding place. She'd looped a whistle around her neck on a yellow cord. When she was sure no one had followed her, Amanda raised the whistle to her lips and blew three short blasts.

She was answered by the honk of a horn. A big smile spread across her face as Pepper's yellow Mustang rolled into view.

"Boy, am I glad to see you!" Amanda huffed as she dropped the bike into the backseat of the convertible and hopped in front. "That burst of speed nearly killed me."

"Did it work?" Pepper asked.

"Yeah." Amanda grinned. "I think they were impressed with the new messenger."

"Here, put this on." Pepper handed Amanda a

cowboy hat and a pair of sunglasses. "We don't want anybody to recognize you."

Amanda put the hat on her head and faced her friend. "How do I look?"

"Divine." Pepper slipped the car into first gear. "Where to?"

"Just a second." Amanda looked down at the invoice Mick had given her. There was a brief note at the bottom.

Mandy, I was a jerk. I'm sorry. Here are the addresses for Ty's and Cynthia's deliveries. Go for it.—M.

"Way to go, Mr. Soul," Amanda murmured to herself. She looked up from the note as a cyclist whipped by them.

"That's Cynthia!" Amanda cried. "Follow her."

"What about your delivery?" Pepper asked.

"It can wait."

Pepper hit the gas pedal and the yellow Mustang rounded the corner with a squeal of tires. Amanda peered over the sunglasses at her friend. "We're supposed to be sneaky, remember?"

"Sorry," Pepper said sheepishly. "I guess I've been watching too many chase scenes in movies."

Pepper maneuvered the car through the thick traffic, struggling to keep the rider in view. Cynthia ran a yellow light that turned red just as the Mustang pulled up to it. Pepper slammed on her brakes and screeched to a halt inside the crosswalk. She slipped the car into reverse and backed up.

"At this rate we'll never be able to follow her," Amanda groaned as they waited for the light to turn green.

"Let me see that address again," Pepper said, taking the note from Amanda. "Portsmouth Square. We'll just meet her there."

When they reached the square, Amanda spotted Cynthia's bike chained to a mailbox in front of a drab office building.

"I can't believe it," Pepper said as she pulled into a loading zone a short distance away.

"What?" Amanda asked.

"Someone stole Cynthia's front wheel. Now why wouldn't they just take the whole bike?"

Amanda stared at her friend and burst out laughing. "Cynthia took her own wheel. All the riders do that to keep people from stealing them."

"Pretty clever, but I hope she knows how to put it back on," Pepper muttered.

Before Amanda could explain, she spotted Cynthia coming out of a brick office building. "That's her. Duck!"

Both girls slumped down into the seat, and Pepper adjusted the rearview mirror so they could keep an eye on Cynthia.

"So that's her," Pepper said as they watched Cynthia pop the front wheel back onto her bike, unlock her chain, and loop it around her neck.

"Yeah," Amanda grumbled. "She's cute, isn't she?"

Pepper shrugged. "If you like petite girls with perfect figures and turned-up noses."

"I think Mick does." Amanda checked the address Mick had given her. "Hey, wait a minute. She just came out of the wrong building." Amanda pointed to a marble building with a striped awning across the square. "She was supposed to make a pickup over there."

"Is that strange?" Pepper asked as they watched Cynthia stuff a manila envelope into her blue nylon backpack.

"Well, it means she's made an unscheduled stop and—wait!" Amanda sat up straight. "Did you see that?"

The two girls bumped heads trying to look in the mirror at the same time.

"Something just fell out of her pack," Amanda said. "What do you think it is?"

Pepper rubbed her head. "I'll go see."

"You can't just go out there," Amanda said, grabbing Pepper by the arm. "Cynthia might see you."

"So what if she does?" Pepper was already out of the car. "She doesn't know me from Adam."

Amanda watched as Pepper strolled up to the mailbox and made a big show of reading the pickup times posted on the drop slot. At the same time she put her foot over the note lying on the ground.

Cynthia didn't notice Pepper at all. She looped her leg over her bike and slipped back into the flow of traffic.

Pepper snatched up the note and raced back to the car. Leaping over the door, she handed the folded piece of paper to her friend.

Amanda could hardly contain her excitement. She'd caught Cynthia making an unscheduled stop, and now she had the evidence to prove the girl was up to no good. "This will show Mick who's jealous, and who's a good detective," she said under her breath.

She carefully unfolded the note and flattened it out on her lap. Amanda read the message three times before finally muttering, "I don't believe it."

"What?" Pepper exclaimed.

"I just don't believe it." Amanda took off her cowboy hat and tossed it into the backseat.

"Let me see that." Pepper grabbed the note and read it out loud. " 'Dear J and L, we'll need three boxes of paper clips tomorrow.' " Pepper looked up in confusion. "Who's J and L?"

"It's an office supply store. A lot of the businesses in this area use it." Amanda leaned back in her seat and groaned. "Boy, do I feel stupid!"

Pepper chuckled softly. "Wait till Mick hears how we nailed old Cynthia."

Amanda sat bolt upright. "Pepper Larson, if you ever breathe a word of this to him, I'll never speak to you again!"

Pepper held up her hands in protest. "Relax.

Your secret is safe with me." She eased the car into traffic. "Where to now?"

"The Embarcadero Center. I still have some deliveries to make. And then . . ." Amanda sighed heavily. "For falsely suspecting Cynthia, I think we should take this to J and L Office Supply." She held up the folded note. "It's the least I can do."

CHAPTER EIGHT

Amanda slid open the door to J & L Office Supply and stepped into the tiny store. A little bell tinkled in the back of the crowded room. Stacks of paper, envelopes, and bulk supplies were piled in every available space. There was barely enough room for her to stand. Amanda waited patiently at the counter but no one came to help her. Finally she called, "Anyone there?"

After a moment a balding man with thick glasses and bushy eyebrows emerged from the back of the store. "What?" he said grumpily.

"I've got an order for you." Amanda dropped the piece of paper on the counter.

The man stared at it for a long time, then said, "Where'd you get this?"

"It's all right," Amanda said. "I'm with Fleet

Street. Cynthia Spartaro asked me to drop it off for her. She got hung up in traffic."

"She did, huh. When?" The man squinted at her suspiciously. Amanda felt so guilty that she didn't dare tell him she had been following Cynthia and watched her drop the note. Instead she said, "This order came in late and Cyn asked me to bring it to you, since I was already riding in this direction."

The man tucked the note in his pocket and picked up a pen. "And your name is?"

"It doesn't matter, I just—"

"Your name, please. I like to keep accurate records of what comes in and goes out of my store."

"Amanda Hart."

The man grunted and went back into the rear of the store.

"Did you give him the order?" Pepper asked when Amanda joined her at the car.

"Yeah," Amanda grumbled, "but he didn't seem very grateful about it."

"I don't blame him," Pepper replied. "With dinky little orders like three boxes of paper clips he won't be in business very long."

"That must be it." Amanda nodded.

Pepper started to pull away from the curb when a shrill whistle cut through the air. She slammed on the brakes, narrowly missing a cyclist who veered around the front of the Mustang. Pepper hit her horn and screamed, "What do you think—"

Amanda clapped her hand across her friend's mouth. "Don't say anything. That's Tyrone Waters."

Pepper narrowed her eyes at her friend. When Amanda removed her hand, Pepper hissed, "I don't care who that is. This is a one-way street and he is going the wrong way!"

Amanda watched Tyrone wheel his bike up to J & L Office Supply and said under her breath, "I think we can agree that all bike messengers are maniacs on wheels, but it doesn't do us a bit of good for you to scream at him and blow our cover."

Before Pepper could respond, Tyrone was out of the store and back on the street. He shoved several packages into his pack, checked his watch, then pedaled down the back street.

The yellow Mustang crept along after him for three city blocks, past dumpsters and rusting fire escapes. The low roar of the muffler seemed unnaturally loud in the cramped street.

"If we're trying to be sneaky," Pepper muttered to Amanda, "this is not the way to do it. All he has to do is look over his shoulder once to know we're following him."

Amanda motioned for Pepper to stop. Tyrone had dismounted and walked down a basement stairwell. Amanda hopped out of the convertible and ordered, "Wait for me. I'm going to see where he went."

She scurried along the road, keeping close to the wall. Amanda ducked behind several large trash cans near the stairwell. She squinted at the heavy door just visible at the bottom of the steps. A freshly stenciled sign had been painted across the peeling door. She read the words out loud softly: "Midnight Express." There was some smaller lettering underneath, and she was leaning forward to get a closer look when the door rattled and opened.

Amanda leaped back into her hiding place just as Tyrone appeared. He was carrying an extra bag, a black nylon pack, which he looped over his other shoulder. Once he'd mounted his bike and turned the corner onto the main road, Amanda ran back to join Pepper.

"It's very strange," she said, leaping into the front seat. "Now he's carrying two messenger bags. Oh, and remind me to check the yellow pages for a business called Midnight Express."

"Boy, Tyrone is fast," Pepper whistled under her breath as she pursued the speeding rider. "It's going to be hard to follow him. He's worse than Cynthia."

"I've got an idea. Get a couple of blocks ahead of him and stop. Then I'll get on my bike and pretend like I've just run into him and see what he's up to."

"No problem."

Pepper hit the accelerator and they whizzed past him up the hill. At the top she pulled over to the curb and Amanda hurriedly lifted her ten-speed out of the backseat.

"Pull out ahead," Amanda said, "and try to keep sight of us in your rearview mirror."

When Tyrone sped by her, she leaped onto the seat and pumped furiously to catch up. Tyrone was obviously winded from the hill because he was coasting.

"Hi," Amanda called out brightly as she came up beside him.

Tyrone looked over at her in surprise, then burst into a broad smile. "Hi, yourself. Things working out?"

Amanda smiled confidently. "Just super." She nodded at the two packs he had slung over his shoulders and whistled. "Looks like you've got a full plate this morning."

Tyrone shook his head. "Naw. One of these has my workout clothes in it. I've got a hot half-court game at the Y after work."

"You can play basketball after riding all day on a bike?"

"Hey, they don't call me the Iron Man for nothing," Tyrone replied with a laugh.

A pedestrian was jaywalking in the crosswalk ahead of them and Amanda instinctively swerved to avoid him. Unfortunately she veered right into Tyrone and their rear wheels locked together.

"What are you doing?" he shouted. There was a squeal of brakes as the bikes collided and the two cyclists were tossed to the ground.

A sharp pain shot through Amanda's knee and wrist as she hit the street and skidded toward the sidewalk. She lay on her stomach, trying to figure out what had happened. Finally Amanda raised her arm. A long red scrape stretched from her elbow all the way to her wrist. She rolled over into a sitting position and saw that little bits of gravel were imbedded in her knee.

"Ow!" Amanda cried as she brushed gingerly at her bleeding skin.

A few feet away Tyrone stood checking the frame of his bike. He turned to face her and shouted, "That was the stupidest move I've ever seen." She watched him hurriedly scoop up the contents of his bags, which were scattered across the pavement. "Where'd you learn to ride a bike, anyway?"

"I was trying to avoid hitting that pedestrian."

Tyrone shook his head in disgust. "Riders like you are a menace."

"Menace?" Amanda felt as if she'd been slapped. "I've watched you run stoplights and break every rule in the book. How dare you call *me* a menace!" Amanda tried to get to her feet and winced in pain.

Tyrone must have seen the look on her face because his voice softened as he said, "I don't mean to get on your case, Amanda. But the rules are different on the street. Are you okay?"

Amanda blinked back angry tears that were threatening to appear and nodded.

Tyrone checked his watch. "I hate to leave you like this, but if I don't make this delivery, the client will have my tail in a sling." Tyrone slung both bags over his shoulders, got on his bike, and as he rode off, she heard him call, "I'll see you back at Fleet Street."

"Mandy, are you hurt?" a voice cried out beside her. It was Pepper, her tousled red bangs framing her worried eyes.

"A little bruised," Amanda admitted, limping over to her fallen bike.

"Is this what you meant by running into him?" Pepper cracked.

Amanda grinned ruefully. "Not quite." She reached over to pick up her bicycle and noticed a small cardboard box lying beneath the spokes. "I can't believe this!" Amanda exclaimed. "This is the second person who's left a delivery behind. How do they stay in business when they're so careless?" She picked up the box, which was filled with little bottles of liquid paper, and examined the address. "J and L Office Supply. It figures."

"What should we do with that?" Pepper asked.

"Well, I'm certainly not going to ride back to J and L." Amanda stuffed the small package into her nylon bag. "I'll take it to Fleet Street. If Ty wants it, he can get it there. Otherwise the office has a free lifetime supply of Wite-Out."

As Amanda walked her bike over to the car, Pepper said, "Listen, we've still got a few days of spring break left—why don't you come skiing with me?"

Amanda bit her lip. "Boy, I'd love to, but . . ."

"But what?" Pepper interrupted. "As far as I can tell, this big *case* you've been working on is going nowhere."

"It sure seems like it right now," Amanda said with a sigh. "I feel bad that I haven't really helped Mick."

"Are you kidding?" Pepper put her hands on her hips. "You've saved his life. He got a bike messenger who is willing to work all hours and cripple herself for free! What have you gotten?"

"Sore muscles." Amanda looked at the purplish red bruise on her arm and the long scrape on her knee, then added, "And a bloody leg."

"Right." Pepper hopped into the front seat of her Mustang. "So it's settled. You're coming with me."

Amanda laughed. "You're pretty convincing, Pepper, but I promised Mick and I'm going to stick with it."

Pepper shoved her glasses up on her nose and stared at her friend. Finally she shrugged. "Oh, well. It's your life."

"Thanks, Pepper," Amanda said with a smile. "For all of your help." She looped her leg over the bike and settled onto the seat.

"You're not going to *ride* back to Fleet Street, are you?" Pepper asked incredulously.

"Coast, is more like it," Amanda replied. "It's all downhill from here. Besides, I have to keep up the appearance of being an ace cyclist."

Pepper rolled her eyes. "Well, *I'm* going home

to check the weather report. And with any luck, you won't see me tomorrow."

Amanda waved good-bye. As she pulled gingerly into traffic, she heard Pepper shout, "Pray for snow!"

CHAPTER NINE

Once she was back at Fleet Street, Amanda slammed her bike into the stand outside and mumbled, "Good riddance!" The rusted metal rack rattled with the blow, and a little white paper bag leaning against it fell over on the ground. It looked like someone's lunch. Amanda bent over to retrieve it but changed her mind.

"I'm tired of picking up after these guys," she declared. "Whoever owns this can pick it up himself." Amanda smoothed her dark hair back into its ponytail and straightened her tam, then limped up the steps, wincing at her newly scraped knee.

"Be still, my beating heart," Charlie gasped melodramatically as she stepped through the door. "It's Amanda!" He flashed her a warm smile and waved her over. "C'mon and join the party."

Cynthia, who was perched on the arm of the beat-up couch, said, "Phil's showing off again."

Phil Wilayto stood in the center of the room, juggling two oranges and an apple. Every time he caught the apple he took a bite out of it.

Amanda was startled to see Tyrone lounging against one of the water pipes. *I thought he had more deliveries to make,* Amanda thought to herself suspiciously. *So how could he get back here ahead of me?* Either Tyrone was an incredibly fast messenger, or he had lied to her.

"Here, catch!" Tyrone tossed a bicycle wrench at Phil, who caught it expertly and flipped the apple core back in Ty's direction.

Charlie Driscoll threw his head back and laughed. "Watch it, Philly boy, don't take a bite out of that wrench. You'll chip your teeth!"

Everyone seemed to be getting along just fine. Even Cynthia had smiled at her when she came in the door. Amanda stood awkwardly by the side of the couch, unsure of how to interpret this new atmosphere at Fleet Street.

"Sit down, Mandy." Charlie patted the seat beside him on the sofa. "I won't bite."

"He's really good," Amanda said as she gratefully sank down into the cushions.

"Not bad," Gabe responded from the curtained door leading into the front of the grocery. "Two oranges and a wrench is okay. But can he handle a box of graham crackers?"

Gabe flipped the box over Phil's head and Cynthia shouted, "Yo, Phil! Behind you."

Phil reached behind his back and caught the box without looking and everyone applauded. Gabe shook his head in amazement. "That man is scary. He's got eyes in the back of his head."

Phil answered by tossing the box back at Gabe. "Have a cracker. It's on me." It hit him squarely in the chest and fell to the ground.

Charlie whipped a dollar bill out of his pocket. "A buck says he can't handle the next thing thrown at him."

"You're on." Tyrone pulled a dollar out of the zipper pocket on his pantleg. "This dude can handle anything."

Cynthia tossed another bill onto the pile on the couch. "I'm with Tyrone."

All eyes turned toward Amanda. "Well, you in?" Charlie asked.

She searched her pockets, then remembered she had some change in her nylon bag. Amanda watched Phil, who was standing on one leg and easily looping the oranges under his lifted leg. "Okay," she said, laughing. "I'm in. A dollar says he can do it."

Charlie collected the money, expertly snapping the bills into a smooth, neat stack in his hand. "Gabe?" he arched an eyebrow at the hulking figure leaning against the desk. "The pot's light."

"Okay, okay." Gabe pulled a crumpled bill out

of his hip pocket and tossed it in Charlie's direction. "My money's on Phil."

"So's mine." Without pausing, Phil pulled a dollar out of his shirt pocket and flipped it to Charlie.

"All right!" Charlie ran his thumb across the pile of bills and declared, "Pot's right." Then he reached for the tiny umbrella protruding from his pack. "Here, Phil, catch this!"

In a single move he slipped it out of the blue nylon knapsack and tossed it at the juggler. As he did, he pressed the release and the umbrella popped open just as Phil was reaching for it. Not only did the canopy fan open, but the plastic handle extended a foot in the other direction. It took Phil completely by surprise.

"Look out," Tyrone shouted as Phil staggered back against one of the posts. The soft canopy flopped against Phil's face and fell to the floor, along with the wrench and the oranges.

"Not fair!" Cynthia said as she hopped off the arm of the couch in protest. "You didn't say you were going to open the umbrella."

"I never said I wouldn't. The bet was that he couldn't juggle it—and he didn't."

"Aw, man," Tyrone complained, "you took us for a ride."

Phil was wincing from where the wrench had fallen on his toe. "I can juggle umbrellas open or closed. I just can't handle them in-between. Give me another chance."

Charlie, who was tucking the money into his

pocket, paused in midair. "All right. I'll give everybody another chance—a chance to double your money."

"What do you want me to juggle?" Phil asked, hopping from one leg to the other like a tennis player waiting to receive a serve. "I'm ready."

"Nothing, my friend." Charlie flashed a wide grin. "This is a whole new ball game."

Tyrone and Cynthia looked at him suspiciously.

Charlie patted the wad of bills in his hands. "All this money says I can go out that door and return with an order of egg rolls from the Golden Dragon in less than three minutes."

"No way!" Tyrone hooted. "It'll take you at least ten minutes to get over there and back."

"What kind of egg rolls?" Cynthia asked.

"Shrimp," Charlie replied without batting an eyelash.

Cynthia chuckled. "Shrimp takes them forever." She tossed another dollar at him. "We won't see you for twenty minutes."

Phil stepped forward and snapped a ten-dollar bill under Charlie's nose. "I go to the Golden Dragon at least four times a week. Even if you sprouted wings and flew, you couldn't get your order and get back here in three minutes. In fact . . ." He reached into his wallet and pulled out a twenty. "In fact, I'm so sure, I'll put all my money on it."

There was a chorus of oohs and aahs from the others. Charlie picked up the twenty and shrugged.

"Brave man." Then he turned to Amanda. "What about you?"

"I'll sit this one out." Amanda didn't add that she'd left her purse in Pepper's car and was flat broke.

"In that case . . ." Charlie snapped the bills taut. "We'll make you the treasurer." He handed her the money, then took off his watch and gave that to her as well. "Plus the official timekeeper." Charlie stood up and walked to the door. "Just say when, and I'll see you in three."

Amanda waited for the second hand to reach twelve and then she shouted, "Go!"

Charlie went out the door just as Mick was coming in. "What's going on?"

"Man, you missed out," Tyrone called.

"On what?" Mick asked as he tossed his pack onto a hook by the lockers.

"On a chance to stick it to your cousin," Gabe told him.

Mick frowned. "What's he done now?" Mick sat down at the desk and leafed through some mail.

"That guy took us on the first bet," Cynthia explained, "but we're going to get him back."

"Bet?" Mick raised an eyebrow. "You've been betting money?" He ran his hand through his hair. "That's not a good idea. Not with Charlie Driscoll."

"Don't worry." Gabe explained what had happened with the juggling.

"Now we're going to double our money," Tyrone cut in. "That fool thinks he can ride to the

Golden Dragon, get an order of egg rolls, and be back here in less than three minutes."

"Did Charlie make the bet?" Mick asked.

Everyone nodded.

Mick shook his head. "Then he can do it. Don't ask me how, but Charlie never bets unless he can win."

"Two minutes and thirty seconds," Amanda announced. She hadn't taken her eyes off the dial.

Tyrone clapped his hands with glee. "Only thirty seconds to go. He hasn't even gotten to the Golden Dragon's door." He chuckled and added, "Plus he forgot about the lunch rush."

"Fifteen seconds."

All eyes were glued to the door as they all joined the countdown.

"Ten. Nine. Eight."

Mick just shook his head. "You'll be sorry."

"Three. Two—"

The door swung open and banged against the wall. "I won!" Charlie burst into the room, holding a white paper bag over his head in triumph. "Four egg rolls, with a side of hot mustard and spicy sauce."

The four riders stared at him dumbfounded.

"Th—that's impossible," Tyrone stammered.

"I don't believe it!" Phil yanked the bag out of Charlie's hands and reached inside. He turned the bag upside down and the egg rolls rolled out onto Mick's desk.

"Believe it and weep," Charlie said pleasantly.

One of the egg rolls fell into Mick's lap. "Hey, watch it." He scooped it up and put it back on the desk. "Man, these are stone cold. What's with that place? Don't they believe in warming the food?"

A light went on in Amanda's head. She squinted at the little white bag suspiciously.

"It's just not possible," Cynthia murmured stubbornly. "Nobody can walk out that door and get back here with an order of egg rolls in three minutes."

Amanda's voice cut through the stillness. "They can, if they bought them earlier, then left them outside leaning against the bike rack."

Charlie spun around and stared at her. A slow smile curled his lips. "No fair giving away my secrets. I thought you were on my side."

"What?" Phil Wilayto grabbed Charlie by the shoulder and spun him around. "Give me my thirty bucks. You cheated."

Charlie looked at Phil evenly. "I did not." He brushed Phil's hand off his shoulder. "Remember what the bet was."

Phil was getting angrier by the second. "I bet all the money I had for this week—"

"That he'd go out that door and return in three minutes with an order of egg rolls from the Golden Dragon," Cynthia finished for him. Her voice was a flat monotone. "He never said he was going *to* the Golden Dragon. He just said the egg rolls would be *from* there."

Tyrone fell back against the couch and started to chuckle. "Man, we were set up *again.*" He held out his hand and gave Charlie a low five. "Slick, my friend, very slick."

"We were ready to play him for a sucker." Cynthia smiled ruefully. "Looks like the joke's on us. Charlie won, fair and square."

"You call that fair?" Phil protested. "He planned it from the beginning. He got us to bet on the juggling so he could take our money with his egg roll scam." Phil narrowed his eyes angrily. "You're nothing but a thief. And I want my money back." Phil lunged at Charlie but Mick caught his hand and stopped him.

"What's going on with you?" he demanded. "Last week you're broke and desperately in need of an advance. Today you're tossing thirty bucks around like it was nothing."

"I wasn't tossing it around," Phil grumbled, rubbing his sore wrist. "It was a sure thing. Anyone would've bet on that."

"There's no such thing as a sure thing," Charlie declared as he calmly counted his money. He paused and grinned at Phil. "That lesson cost you some money, but someday you'll thank me."

"Thank you? I'm going to kill you!" Phil lunged again and this time Gabe stepped between them. Mick helped him hustle Phil over to the corner.

"I don't know what's with you," Mick said in a low voice, "but we don't put up with that stuff."

Gabe nodded. "Not here. So sit down and chill out."

"You can't push me around," Phil shouted. He pulled away and rushed over to his locker. Mick started to follow when the phone rang.

Mick sat back down at the desk. "Fleet Street. Talk to me." He took the call and shouted, "I've got two orders. Tyrone, Phil—you're up."

"Forget it," Phil snapped over his shoulder. "I've got a dentist's appointment." He slammed the locker shut and stormed out the door.

Mick shrugged casually. "Charlie, it's yours."

"Yo." Charlie grabbed his bag and leaped to his feet.

As Tyrone passed the desk, he scooped up an egg roll and showed it to Charlie. "You don't mind if I take this? I figure I paid for it."

"Go ahead, take 'em all," Charlie replied as the boys headed for the door. "I hate cold egg rolls."

Mick answered two more calls, then stood up and stretched. Amanda watched in stunned amazement. Mick was acting as if nothing strange had happened. Charlie had just proved he was a major con artist, Phil had gone berserk, and now it seemed as if everything were business as usual. She shook her head and thought, "If he doesn't care, I don't either."

She stepped forward to tell Mick she was quitting just as the phone rang again.

"Gabe, will you get that?" Mick said, strolling over to join Amanda. "I happen to know that Phil saw the dentist last week and his teeth were fine," he whispered. "Take the next order, and I'll meet you around the corner. We've got to follow him."

"Who's up?" Gabe shouted, waving a yellow dispatch.

Before she knew what she was doing, Amanda shouted, "I've got it."

Seconds later Amanda met Mick in the alley. She'd forgotten all about quitting and was anxious to continue with the case.

"Come on." Mick pointed toward the figure pedaling off into the distance. "Phil's getting away. We need to follow him."

She reached for her ten-speed and Mick shouted, "Forget that. We don't need to waste energy pedaling all over town." He put his fingers to his lips and blew a loud whistle at a passing cab.

The car screeched to a halt, Mick threw open the passenger door, and the two of them hopped inside. Mick leaned forward and barked, "Follow that bike!"

CHAPTER TEN

Pull over here.

The cabdriver obeyed Mick's command and stopped in front of one of the nightclubs on Broadway. Mick tossed a few bills on the front seat and he and Amanda scrambled out onto the pavement.

Even though it was still afternoon, Broadway was already gearing up for another round of nightlife. Neon lights flashed above the shoddy nightclubs and bars. Brash barkers dressed in cheap satin tuxedo jackets stood in the doorways, urging passersby to come inside. A half a block away they watched Phil turn his bike into an alley adjoining a club with a purple-and-lime-striped awning.

"Where's he going?" Amanda asked as the two of them hurried down the sidewalk after their prey.

"That's The Last Laff," Mick replied. "It's been around for years. Comedy, cabaret stuff. They get a few up-and-comers in there but mostly has-beens."

A big tear stretched down the center of the faded awning. "Looks pretty sleazy to me," Amanda said.

As they stepped over a drunk who lay slumped on the sidewalk, Mick said, "It is." He grabbed her hand and pulled her toward the entrance. "Come on."

"We can't go in there," Amanda hissed. "We're underage." She pointed to the bouncer standing guard at the door. He was a big beefy guy with slicked-back hair and an ill-fitting dinner jacket of shiny red material with black lapels. A huge, matching red bow tie hung crookedly from his collar. "He'll never let us in."

"Relax." Mick flipped up the collar of his leather jacket and grinned. "You're with me, remember? I'll get us in."

"But look at me." She gestured to her outfit. "I'm dressed like a bike messenger, not a girl on the town."

Mick studied her carefully. "These joints don't care what you wear. But you do look a little young." He reached up and undid the clip holding her hair in a ponytail. "Shake your head."

Amanda followed his instructions and her thick, dark hair fell loosely down around her shoulders. "Much better," Mick murmured.

He grabbed her by the hand and swaggered up

to the doorman, slipping a ten-dollar bill into his palm. "Table for two by the band, my man."

The doorman's hand closed over the money. "You're in. And don't cause any trouble." He flipped back a heavy green curtain and they stepped into the darkened hall of the nightclub. It took a moment for Amanda's eyes to adjust.

A tired-looking woman sat on a stool with her legs crossed, reading a movie magazine. She was wearing a black satin miniskirt and a tight black T-shirt with the words THE LAST LAFF written across her chest in glitter. Her peroxided hair was swept up into a stiff hairdo that seemed to defy gravity.

When she saw them, the woman set the magazine on the counter and pushed herself to her feet. Without smiling she muttered, "Follow me."

As the hostess led them down the darkened corridor, Mick whispered, "How much hairspray do you think it takes to keep her hair up like that?"

"Hairspray?" Amanda giggled. "I'll bet she uses a gallon of shellac."

"Pick any empty table," the hostess said, parting a beaded curtain at the end of the corridor. "They're plenty of 'em."

Tables had been scattered across the smoke-filled room, with tiny lamps at the center of each making a pool of yellowish light. Small groups of people sat at a few of the tables, but most of the tables were empty. Along the far side of the room a bar stretched the entire length of the wall. A bartender leaned against the mirror, halfheartedly wiping glasses and slipping them onto the sliding racks that hung above his head.

On stage a belly dancer was gyrating to a scratchy record. The whining cry of the desert flutes gave Amanda a headache.

"I don't see a sign of Phil anywhere," Amanda whispered as she peered out over the darkened room.

"He's got to be here someplace," Mick replied. "We saw him come in. Maybe he's at one of the tables in front, or over there." He pointed to the high-backed booths along the opposite wall.

Amanda, trying to act as if she went to clubs like this all the time, casually draped her elbow over the back of her chair and swiveled to look in the direction of the booths. She nearly fell out of her seat as she whispered, "Mick!"

"What?" Mick leaned forward intently. "Do you see Phil?"

"Not him. Someone else." Amanda spun her chair back around and keeping her head down, hissed, "Don't look."

Mick put his arm around her shoulder and leaned his face close to hers. "Who did you see?"

"Your cousin."

"Charlie?" Mick barked.

Amanda put her finger to his lips. "Hush!"

"Are you sure?" Mick lowered his voice to a hoarse whisper.

She nodded.

"Stay down. I don't want him to see us." Mick grabbed her arm and pulled her under the table. The force of his movement sent both of their chairs rolling away from the table on their casters. One bumped the next table and crashed to the floor.

"Subtle," Amanda said wrily. "Very subtle."

"What the hell is Charlie doing here?" Mick said, peering over the tabletop. "I'll bet he's up to no good. And *that's* a bet I'd put money on."

Amanda's knee started to throb from where she had scraped it earlier. "Well, hiding under this table is not going to tell us anything."

"What's going on?" a nasal voice demanded. "We don't put up with any funny business here."

They peered out from beneath the table to see a heavyset waitress training a flashlight on them.

"I lost a contact lens," Amanda replied, thinking quickly.

Amanda noticed that the woman was wearing the same outfit and hairdo as the woman who'd seated them. But this woman looked twenty years older. Amanda wondered if she was really that old or if working in a place like this just made her look that way.

The waitress focused the beam of the light on Amanda's face. "Hey, how old are you, anyway? Let me see some ID."

Amanda squinted and covered her eyes with her fingers. "I—uh, lost it."

"Along with your contact lens? Sure." The waitress turned and shouted toward the bar. "Louie! We've got some minors here."

"Hey, hold on a minute." Mick straightened up indignantly. "We're guests of Phil Wilayto's."

"Never heard of him," the woman shot back. "Get them out of here, Louie."

A short, pudgy man dressed in a rumpled suit hurried over and grabbed each of them by the arm and pulled them to their feet. His grip was like a steel vise. Amanda barely had time to grab her pack off the table before he'd dragged them out into the corridor.

"Get your hands off her," Mick protested as they neared the front door.

"This is no place for kids," the guy growled. He swept back the heavy curtain and shoved them outside. "Come back when you grow up."

Mick and Amanda stood for a moment in stunned silence, blinking into the afternoon light. Finally Mick turned to her and said sheepishly, "I'm sorry about that. I just didn't expect to see my cousin in there. I guess I overreacted a little."

Amanda raised an eyebrow. "A little?"

"You okay?" Mick asked, placing his hand on her arm.

Amanda tried to smile. "Yes. Embarrassed, but okay."

Mick straightened his collar and combed back his hair with his fingers. "Well, we did find out a couple of things from our little visit."

"Like?"

"Phil and Charlie are hanging out on Broadway when they're supposed to be delivering messages for me. "And"—he grinned crookedly—"they've got lousy taste in nightclubs."

Amanda began to chuckle, but the laughter died in her throat as two men in overcoats suddenly appeared behind Mick. Before she could say a word they grabbed him by the collar and dragged him into the alley.

"We warned you, punk," one of the thugs snarled as he shoved Mick against the wall. "You're in the wrong business. But you don't seem to get the message."

"Maybe this will help you remember," the other man said. He slammed his fist into Mick's stomach.

Amanda saw Mick crumple up in pain and a wave of white-hot fury swept over her. Without thinking, she leaped into the alley and swung her pack at the head of the man who'd hit Mick. "You leave him alone," she yelled. "I'm calling the police."

"Yeow!" the hood cried as the pack hit him in the back of the neck. Amanda swung it again, but the other thug caught the bag by its straps, wrenched it out of her hands, and flung it across the alley.

That didn't stop Amanda. Her adrenaline was charging through her body and she flailed at the man with her fists, screaming, "Police! Police!"

He caught her by the wrists and put his face

close to hers. "Yeah, you call the police," he said with a terrible leer. "They'd love to talk to your friend here."

His grip was so painful that her body went limp. Amanda watched helplessly as the other guy drove his fist into Mick's stomach again and growled, "Tomorrow, or you're history."

Mick fell to his knees, choking, as the two men disappeared around the corner. Amanda stumbled over to Mick's side. He sat very still clutching his stomach with his eyes closed.

"Mickey, are you hurt?"

He opened one eye and peered at her. "I'll be okay in a minute." Then a slow smile spread across his face. "You were amazing. What got into you?"

Amanda ran a hand through her hair. "I don't know, I guess I just couldn't stand to see you get hurt."

"Those guys could've had guns."

"I didn't even think about that." Amanda spun around to pick up her bag and got angry all over again. "And look what they did to my pack!"

The top flap was torn open and all the contents had spilled out onto the pavement. She knelt down and began slamming things back into the bag. Amanda picked up the box from J & L Office Supply. It was crumpled and torn from being thrown against the wall, and several bottles of Wite-Out rolled onto the ground. Some of the caps had come off and she was covered in white powder as she picked the bottles up.

"Oh, great. Now I'm going to get this stuff all over the inside of my bag." She reached down and touched the white powder. "Can you believe it?" she said to Mick. "It's all dried up. What a lousy product." She batted at her leg and puffs of white dust billowed up into the air.

Mick knelt soundlessly beside her and held one of the open bottles in his hand.

Amanda waved her hand in the air in front of her and coughed. "This stuff is everywhere."

"Amanda."

Something in Mick's voice made her freeze. "What is it?"

Mick looked over both shoulders and then down at his hands. "I think I just figured out why those hoods are after me."

"Why?"

She watched as he carefully scooped what was left of the powder back into the bottle and dropped it into her pack.

"This isn't Wite-Out," Mick said quietly. "It's cocaine."

CHAPTER ELEVEN

"There are ten bottles of Wite-Out here," Mick said as they spread the contents of Amanda's pack across her bedspread.

When they had discovered what was inside the bottles, Amanda had hurriedly suggested they go to her house. Her relatives had gone to a play that evening and the house was empty. It seemed the safest and most unlikely place to hide. On the way over she explained how she had gotten the box of office supplies in the first place.

Mick lined up the little bottles in a row. They stared at them in amazement.

"How much do you think they're worth?" Amanda asked.

"Per bottle?" Mick held up one of the bottles and read the label. "These hold about fifteen grams each." He shook the bottle and said, "I'd say it's worth about two thousand on the street."

Amanda's jaw fell open. "You mean we've got—?"

Mick nodded. "Twenty thousand dollars' worth of illegal drugs sitting between us."

"Oh, my God." Amanda leaped off the bed. "This is scary, Mick."

"You're telling me. Somebody's going to miss this pretty soon and come looking for it. Then we'll have to do some fast talking to explain how you happened to get it."

"But nobody knows that I have it," Amanda said. "Not even Tyrone. It fell out of his pack. I only found it on the pavement after he'd ridden off."

Mick leaned against the brass headboard of her bed. "Mandy, are you sure this came from Ty's pack?"

Amanda nodded solemnly. "Positive. Pepper and I spotted him leaving J and L Office Supply and decided to follow him."

Mick sat forward. "Where did he go?"

Amanda paced in a nervous circle on the rug, trying to piece together the events that had happened earlier that day. "We followed him in Pepper's Mustang down a back street. He went inside a basement. I thought then that it was an odd spot to deliver office supplies."

"Can you remember the name of the place?"

She squeezed her eyes shut, trying to remember the lettering she'd seen on the door. "Midnight . . . something like that."

"Think!" Mick urged. "That may be where he was supposed to make the drop."

"No." Amanda shook her head. "He was making another pickup. He went in with one sack and came out with another—a black one. It had some lettering on it." She snapped her fingers. "Midnight Express. That's it."

Mick cocked his head. "Never heard of it. Sounds like a phony business."

"We can look it up." Amanda moved to her desk and pulled a San Francisco Yellow Pages out of the drawer. She tossed the heavy book to Mick.

As he slipped through the business section of the directory, he said, "Midnight Express is probably some front for Tyrone's drug deals."

Amanda pointed to the cardboard box marked J & L Office Supply. "What does J and L have to do with it?"

Mick shrugged. "Probably nothing. Ty picked up the box of real Wite-Out from them, took the bottles to Midnight Express, then made the switch there." Mick slammed the directory shut. "It's not listed."

"Maybe it's a new number. I'll call information." Amanda picked up the elegant white-and-gold French phone her parents had given her for her birthday and dialed.

The operator gave her the number and she hastily scribbled it on a pad by the phone. As she dialed, Mick came up to the desk and put his ear by the receiver. It rang twice, then she heard a hissing sound and a familiar voice intoned, "Thank you for calling Midnight Express. Our office is open from nine A.M. to five P.M., Monday through Friday. Please leave a short message at the beep."

The moment the tone sounded, Mick grabbed the receiver and shouted, "What the hell do you think you're doing, Tyrone? Are you trying to get us all killed? I want to talk to you, and I want—" Mick looked up suddenly. "I was cut off."

"It's a good thing, too." Amanda took the phone out of his hands and put it down on its cradle. "Now Tyrone knows that we know he's behind the dope dealing."

Mick slumped down on the edge of the bed. "I still can't believe it. Why would he do that?"

"I don't know, but I think we should call the police," Amanda said firmly.

"No way." Mick shook his head. "I'm not turning Ty in. I want to talk to him first.

"Talk to him?" Amanda crossed her arms and stared at Mick dubiously. "Like you did just now on the answering machine?"

"No, no." Mick stood up and paced anxiously around the room. "I want to talk some sense into that stubborn head of his. Ty's my friend. Or at least he was. He's got too much going for him to do something stupid like this."

"I still think we need outside help," Amanda

insisted. "I mean, people are murdered every day for smaller amounts of cocaine than this."

Mick stared at her for a moment, then stood up abruptly. "You're right."

As he picked up the phone, Amanda asked, "Who're you going to call, Sergeant Rubano?" Lou Rubano was a detective on the San Francisco police force. They had come in contact with him on several of their earlier cases.

"I can't call Rubano," Mick said. "Not yet. I want to keep the cops out of this for now."

Amanda watched as Mick dialed a number. "So who are you calling?"

"Gabe."

"Gabe?" Amanda fell back on the bed in exasperation.

"Look, it's his business, too," Mick said. "He's my partner, and he's got a right to know what's going down." As he waited for Gabe to answer, Mick covered the mouthpiece with his hand and said with a grin, "Besides, Gabe's my main man. I'd rather have him behind me in a fight than a thousand cops." Mick suddenly stood up straight. "Evening, Mrs. Sanchez. This is Mick. Can I talk to Gabe a minute?"

There was a long pause. Mick cocked his head and said, "He's not? Where is he? Oh, really. . . . Did he say when he'd be back? Oh." Mick hesitated for a second, then said, "By the way, Mrs. Sanchez, how's your father?"

Amanda watched a little muscle clench in Mick's jaw.

"Oh. Glad to hear it. Well, just tell Gabe I called. Will you do that for me? *Muchas gracias, señora. Hasta luego.*"

Mick placed the receiver in its cradle, then turned and punched the wall with his fist.

Amanda sat up in shock. "Is there something the matter?"

"You're damn right there is. I think I just broke my hand." Mick winced and shook his wrist to get rid of the pain. Amanda moved forward to help but he brushed her aside.

"Gabe's not home. His mom doesn't know where he went, or when he'll be back."

"So?" Amanda looked confused. "That's not unusual, is it?"

"You don't understand. I'd asked him to work with me on the case tonight and he told me he had to stay home to look after his sick grandfather." Mick ran his hand through his hair. "His grandfather's fine. What the *hell* is going on?"

"I don't know," Amanda replied.

"Why would my best friend lie to me?"

Amanda had no answer. Or at least none that she dared voice. Gabe's strange behavior made her worry that maybe somehow he was involved with the whole drug mess.

Mick stood for a long moment with his hands on hips, staring at the floor. Then suddenly he sprang into action. He slipped on his leather jacket and hurriedly tossed the bottles of Wite-Out into the little cardboard box.

"What are you doing?" Amanda exclaimed.

"I'm going outside," he muttered. "I've got to think."

"What are you going to do with that?" She pointed to the cardboard box tucked under his arm.

"I don't know," Mick replied. "Hide it somewhere."

"You're crazy to take it with you," Amanda protested. "I think you should leave it here."

"What?"

"No one's looking for me," she reminded him. "I'll lock it in my uncle's safe. He rarely opens it."

A look of frank admiration crossed his face and he handed her the box. "What would I do without you?" Then he turned and left the room.

"Mick, wait!" Amanda cried. "What about tomorrow?"

"I'll call you," Mick shouted back from the stairs.

She was about to follow him when her phone rang. The sound nearly made her jump out of her skin. She heard the front door close just as she picked up the phone.

"There's snow in them thar hills," Pepper squealed gleefully on the other end of the line.

Amanda sank down on her bed and leaned back

against the pillows. "That's the first good news I've heard all day."

"What happened? Did things get worse after I left you?"

"*Worse* doesn't even begin to describe it."

"Oooh!" Pepper gasped. "I want every awful detail."

Amanda opened her mouth to speak. She wanted to tell Pepper about her bizarre experience at The Last Laff, the two awful hoods who beat Mick up, and the horrible discovery of the cocaine—but something inside made her stop. Telling Pepper would involve her in the whole mess and maybe even endanger her life.

"Listen, Pepper, I can't really talk right now," Amanda said carefully. "But if anything happens to me, just remember this—the answer's in Uncle Silas's safe."

There was a short pause, and then Pepper shrieked, "What do you mean, if something happens to you? What's going on here, Amanda Hart?"

"I'm not sure," Amanda replied. "But when I find out, I'll let you know. Just remember what I told you—"

"The answer's in Uncle Silas's safe?" Pepper repeated. "What's that? Some kind of code?"

Amanda bit her lip. "I'm sorry, Pepper, but I really can't say. Just have a good time on your ski trip and I'll see you Monday."

"Amanda!"

"Bye, Pepper!" Amanda sang out cheerfully. "Happy shooshing." Amanda hung up the phone and mumbled, "Or whatever it is they call it when you go down those slopes."

She stared down at the cardboard box filled with the deadly drug. It felt like a time bomb ticking away in her hands, a time bomb set to go off in twenty-four hours.

Amanda hurried downstairs and placed it in the safe in her uncle's study. She locked the box behind the heavy metal door, wishing she could lock the fear out of her mind the same way.

CHAPTER TWELVE

The next day Amanda hurried to Fleet Street on her white scooter. All night long she'd waited in her room, hoping to hear from Mick, but he hadn't called. She'd waited until two o'clock that afternoon but hadn't heard a word.

Now she was getting worried. What if he had confronted Tyrone, and Ty had become violent? People were killed every day for smaller amounts of drugs that what they'd found.

Amanda shook her head, trying to keep those terrible thoughts away. She turned the throttle and accelerated as fast as she could toward Fleet Street.

A block before she reached the Sanchez Grocery, a figure suddenly leaped onto the road in front of her, waving his arms. Amanda hit the brakes and wobbled to a halt.

"Mick!" she gasped. "What are you trying to do, kill me?"

He rushed to her side and said, "Sorry. I didn't mean to scare you. I just wanted to stop you before you got to Fleet Street." He helped her off the scooter and pulled it up onto the sidewalk.

"What's going on?" Amanda asked. "Where've you been?"

"Shhh!" Mick pulled her back into a doorway. "Stay very still." He gestured with his head toward the street. "They're back!"

Amanda inhaled sharply as a long black limousine slowly cruised by them and turned the corner at the grocery. The tinted windows were so dark, she couldn't see who was inside.

"This is the fourth time they've circled the block." Mick's face looked drawn and haggard. "They were here when I arrived for work this morning."

"Oh, God, Mick," Amanda moaned. "Do you think they've come for the, uh . . . ?" She didn't dare say "cocaine" out loud. "The, uh . . . office supplies?"

Mick shook his head. "I don't think so." Mick squinted across the street to get a better look at the car. "These guys want the dealing to stop. I have a feeling the, um, 'office supplies' belong to a totally different bunch of crooks."

"Then what are they doing here?"

"They gave me till midnight to shut down. This is just a reminder that they mean business. A very visible reminder."

Amanda tugged on his sleeve. "Can't you just explain to them that it's not you who's cutting in on their territory, that you know who is, and you're going to make him stop?"

Mick chuckled humorlessly. "I'd love to. But with these jokers, actions speak louder than words."

The image of the hoods beating Mick in the alley flashed through Amanda's mind once again and she shuddered.

"I've got to get ahold of Ty and put a stop to this today."

"Didn't he come to work?"

"No." Mick jammed his hands in his pockets and stared at his feet. "He must have gotten my message last night. But I can't get an answer at his house."

They wheeled the scooter down the street, sticking close to the shadows of the buildings, until they were directly across from the Sanchez Grocery. Amanda quickly parked and locked the scooter, then stepped back with Mick into a darkened doorway.

"Have you talked to Gabe yet?" Amanda asked, keeping her eyes on the black limousine.

Mick nodded. "Briefly. He called this morning and said he'd be late."

"What? Why?"

"He wouldn't say. Maybe he's with Tyrone.

Maybe the two of them are running the whole drug operation. Maybe everyone at Fleet Street's in on it except me." Mick gestured angrily at the black car. "Maybe they're all sitting in that car right now, plotting how they're going to waste me."

"Maybe your imagination is working overtime." She put her hand on his cheek. "You look worn-out. Why don't we get some coffee and talk this over?"

Mick stood his head. "I can't. Someone's got to be at Fleet Street to take the calls."

"How are you going to get in there when that car's watching the alley?"

"We'll go in through the grocery."

They scurried across the street and slipped in the front of the tiny store. Mick waved at Mr. Sanchez, who was standing behind the cash register, ringing up a customer's order.

The phone was ringing when they stepped through the curtain into the back office. Gabe stood with his back to them, slipping something behind the couch.

"Where the hell have you been?" Mick demanded.

Gabe spun around, nearly losing his balance. Then he gestured toward the phone. "Are you going to get that? Or are you going to let it ring all day?"

Mick reached over and unplugged the phone. "Answer my question."

"I told you I'd be late this morning." Gabe put his hands on his hips and said, "What's got into you, anyway?"

Mick shook his head in amazement. "What's got into me? Since when did you start lying to me?"

Gabe tilted his head. "What are you talking about?"

Mick crossed his arms and glared at his friend. "Tell me where you were last night. I already know you weren't baby-sitting your grandfather."

Gabe dropped his eyes to the floor. "I can't tell you right now," he mumbled. Then he looked up and added, "But I'll explain later. Trust me."

"Trust you?" Mick leaped to his feet angrily. "I can't trust anybody! Our riders aren't showing up, I've been beat up twice for something I know nothing about, a carload of hoods is sitting in a limo outside the door, just itching to get their hands on me again." He slammed a locker door shut with a clang. "And you're talking about trust?"

Amanda watched as Mick stood glaring at his best friend. She had never seen him so upset.

"Okay." Mick threw his hands up in the air. "You want me to trust you? I'll trust you. Take over the business. Mandy and I have things we've got to do."

He didn't wait for Gabe's response. Mick grabbed Amanda by the hand and led her back through the grocery store.

Once they were on the sidewalk, Mick turned

and faced her. "It looks like it's just you and me now," he said grimly. "Come on."

"Where are we going?" Amanda asked as Mick led her over to her white scooter.

"To Tyrone's," Mick replied. "He's got some explaining to do."

Tyrone Waters lived on Haight Street near the panhandle of Golden Gate Park. The address was an old Victorian house that had been converted into several apartments. Tyrone's door was located around the side and up a steep flight of wooden steps.

Mick and Amanda climbed the stairs and Mick rang the doorbell. There was no response. He rang it again. Finally they heard the sound of footsteps behind the door. "Leave me alone," a muffled voice said. "I told you, I don't know anything."

"Tyrone." Mick leaned in close to the door. "It's Mick. Let me in, I've got to—"

"Go away," Tyrone replied. "I can't talk to you right now."

"I don't think he wants visitors," Amanda said as images of Tyrone's getting violent flashed through her head. "Maybe we should come back later." Amanda started to retreat down the steps when Mick put his hand on her shoulder.

"We're going to talk to him now." Mick pounded with his fist on the door. "Open up, Tyrone. I'm not going away until I get some answers. You've been double-crossing me, and I want to know why."

"What are you talking about?" Tyrone said. "I never double-crossed anyone."

"Oh, yeah? What about Midnight Express?"

There was a long silence on the other side of the door. Finally Ty's voice said, "I was planning to tell you about that this morning."

"I'll bet you were." Mick laughed humorlessly.

"Really, I was. And then this happened."

They heard the click of several locks and the sound of a latch being pulled back. The door slid slowly open and Amanda gasped in dismay.

Tyrone's handsome face was covered with deep purple bruises. His eyes were almost swollen shut, and a bloodstained bandage was wrapped over his ear.

"My God." Mick's voice was scarcely a whisper. "Who did it?"

"Get inside, quick."

They hurried into the apartment and Tyrone locked the door behind them.

Amanda surveyed the one-room apartment in dismay. She could see that it had been tastefully decorated, but now it was in shambles. A black lacquer chair lay in splinters beside the small leather couch. The telephone had been pulled out of the wall and the broken pieces littered the carpet. In the kitchen area, the butcher-block table had been knocked over. Broken dishes were scattered across the tiled floor. Bloodstained towels were draped across the sink, with a bottle of iodine and a bag of cotton balls beside them.

"They were here when I got home last night," Tyrone explained, sinking down onto the couch. "Two punks."

"Well-dressed?" Mick cut in. "In suits?"

"No. Street toughs. One of them was wearing a red stocking cap and an old letter jacket. I never got a good look at the other one. He grabbed me from behind."

"What did they want?"

"They kept talking about some package I was supposed to deliver."

" 'Some package'?" Mick mimicked, raising an eyebrow. "I'm sure they were looking for the box of drugs you lost on the street."

"*Drugs?* What are you talking about?"

"Come on, man, be straight with me," Mick snapped. "We know all about Midnight Express."

Tyrone looked totally confused. "I don't read you. Midnight Express is a messenger service. It has nothing to do with drugs."

"A messenger service?" Mick and Amanda repeated in unison.

"Yeah, mine. Like I said, I was going to tell you about it this morning, but those two punks put a cramp in my plans."

Mick cocked his head. "I don't get it."

"I was going into business on my own."

"What about Fleet Street? I thought you liked working with us."

"I do. But I like being my own boss better. I looked at you and Gabe and I thought, that's for me."

Mick leaned against the wall, looking absolutely stunned.

"I wasn't cutting you out, Mick," Tyrone explained quickly. "I let the financial district go completely and concentrated on the firms south of Market Street."

"But how could you ride two jobs?" Amanda asked.

"It wasn't easy," Tyrone admitted with a grin. "But whenever I got behind, I'd call in sick . . ."

"I see." Mick nodded. "Like that sprained ankle?"

"I'm sorry to have lied to you," Tyrone said quietly, "but I needed to make sure my business was going strong before I broke the news."

Tyrone limped over to the refrigerator and pulled out the ice cube tray. He wrapped some ice in a dishtowel and pressed it to his forehead.

"I don't think you'll be making any deliveries for a few days," Amanda remarked.

Tyrone nodded ruefully. "No. My action's in traction for the time being." He picked up one of the kitchen chairs and sat down. "But now you can answer some questions for me. What were these dudes who beat me up looking for?"

"Cocaine," Mick replied, jamming his fists in his pockets. "Lots of it. About twenty thousand dollars' worth."

Tyrone whistled softly through his teeth. "No wonder they almost killed me." He shook his head incredulously. "And it was in my bag? How did it get there?"

"The cocaine was stashed in little bottles of Wite-Out from J and L Office Supply," Amanda explained. "We figured you were taking the real stuff out of the bottles at Midnight Express, then refilling them with cocaine and delivering them to your buyers."

"That's logical enough," Tyrone admitted. "But dead wrong. That delivery I dropped was supposed to have been Phil's."

Amanda and Mick exchanged startled looks.

"He asked me to switch with him at the last minute. He said J and L was out of his way."

"Come on, Amanda," Mick said, moving swiftly toward the door. "Guess who we visit next."

Amanda was already on her feet. She placed her hand on Tyrone's shoulder. "Are you going to be all right here by yourself?"

"I'm going over to my cousin's house in Oakland," he replied, "and lay low for a few days."

"Good idea," Mick said. "I'll call you when we get to the bottom of this thing."

When the two emerged from Ty's apartment, it was late afternoon and daylight was fading fast. While Amanda unlocked her scooter, Mick hurried to a nearby phone booth and called Phil at his home. Moments later he joined Amanda and slid onto the seat beside her.

"Was he there?" she asked, handing Mick his helmet.

"No. His mother said he's at a club in North Beach."

"Not . . . ?" Amanda winced, remembering the awful night club with its torn green-and-purple awning.

"You got it," Mick said. "The Last Laff."

"But we can't go back there," Amanda said. "They'll recognize us and throw us out."

"Not if we go in disguise."

"Disguise?" Amanda repeated. "How are we—?"

"Just leave that to me," Mick replied, wrapping his arms around her waist. "Now let's ride. Time's running out."

CHAPTER THIRTEEN

"I feel absolutely ridiculous in this getup," Amanda muttered as she and Mick hurried down the street toward the nightclub.

"You look great," Mick whispered back. "Take my word for it." He pointed at the their reflection in a storefront window and Amanda groaned.

A pair of bizarre strangers stared back at her. The girl was wearing a tight, red satin minidress, with sleek black hose and red high heels. The guy wore a shiny black double-breasted suit with a black-and-red polka-dot tie that almost glowed in the dark. A thick mustache bristled from beneath the mirrored sunglasses perched on his nose.

"You've got to admit," Mick said, "my friend Tony at the costume shop did a great job on our disguises."

"I still think this wig makes me look like Dolly Parton." Amanda shook her head and a wave of thick, platinum curls tumbled down around her face. "I can't believe I let you talk me into this. It'll never work."

"Sure it will," Mick replied, scratching the mustache glued to his upper lip. "No one would know it was us in a million years."

"You'd better be right." The red pumps she was wearing had four-inch heels, which made Amanda feel as if she were walking around on ice skates. She took a tentative step and wobbled dangerously.

"Whoa!" Mick said, putting his arm around her waist to steady her. "Haven't you ever worn spike heels before?"

"Well . . . they take some getting used to, that's all." She pushed away from him and took a few steps across the pavement.

Mick whistled appreciatively. "They sure make a good pair of legs look great."

"Then you wear them," she retorted. "These shoes must have been designed in a torture chamber."

Mick stopped smiling and stared intently behind them.

"What's the matter?" Amanda asked. "You've been looking over your shoulder ever since we left the costume shop."

"I keep thinking someone's following us." Mick shook his head. "Just nerves, I guess."

Amanda shivered. "Let's hurry up and find Phil. I want to get this over with."

"You and me both. Come on."

The moment they started walking, two scruffy-looking figures stepped out of the shadows across the street. Amanda inhaled sharply. One of them was wearing a red stocking cap and a worn letter jacket.

"Mick!" she whispered. "Are they the ones—"

"Who beat up Ty?" Mick cut in. "They sure match his description."

He took Amanda by the arm and they hurried toward the blinking neon lights of the nightclub where a small crowd stood in line, waiting to get in.

Amanda glanced behind her and saw the two punks weaving in and out of the moving cars toward them. "We'll never get inside in time," Amanda hissed.

"The stage door." Mick pointed to the narrow doorway a few yards down the street from the main entrance. A sign above it announced TALENT NIGHT—ENTER HERE.

"Let's go!" Mick grabbed Amanda by the hand and led her inside the stage door, where a gaunt man stood guard. From behind him the amplified sound of someone talking could be heard, punctuated from time to time with loud laughter.

"What's your act?" he demanded.

"Sorry?" Amanda asked.

"Your act, sister. What do you do? Sing?

Dance?" The man tapped his pen on the clipboard in his hand. "I'm the stage manager. I gotta know, so I can write you in on the schedule."

Amanda stammered helplessly. "I—I, uh, I don't . . ."

"Don't be shy," Mick said brashly. "You know you're the hottest act in the city."

Amanda stared at Mick as if he were crazy.

"The fact is, she can do it all—sing, dance—you name it."

"Oh?" The stage manager looked Amanda up and down in way that made her squirm.

"So where do we go?" Mick demanded.

"We?" The man squinted at him suspiciously. "I thought she was a solo act."

"I'm her manager," Mick declared firmly. "Where she goes, I go."

The man shrugged, then gestured with his thumb down the corridor behind him. "Dressing rooms are that way. Just grab an empty make-up table. Drop your charts in the pit when you go on stage."

"Charts?" Amanda repeated.

"Your sheet music," the man snapped. "Just give them to the piano player. If he doesn't know the tune, he'll fake it. I'll call you in five."

Mick had started to guide a stunned Amanda down the hall when the stage manager shouted after them, "Hey, sugar, you didn't tell me the name of your act."

Amanda turned to Mick, who shrugged helplessly. Then she noticed a vase of withered flowers sitting forlornly outside a dressing-room door.

"Rose," she declared. "Long Stemmed Rose."

Mick grinned. "You got that, buddy?"

"Got it," the man replied, scribbling on his pad. "Long Stemmed Rose."

Mick and Amanda hurried down the corridor. To the right, through a set of black drapes, they could see the bright stage.

"Mick, look!" Amanda nearly fell off her high heels in surprise.

"What?"

She pointed at the stage. "Is that who I think it is?"

Ringed by a circle of light, a wiry figure in a tuxedo was juggling a top hat, a carving knife, and a melon. It was Phil Wilayto.

They watched openmouthed as Phil effortlessly kept the objects dancing in the air, while a steady stream of jokes poured from his mouth. The audience was eating it up.

"You know, he's not bad," Mick said.

"Oliver Twister, the Juggling Jokester." Amanda read the sign placed on a tripod near the edge of the stage. "No wonder no one at the club knew Phil's name."

There was a drum roll and Phil caught the top hat on his head, split the melon in midair with the knife, and then caught the two pieces in each hand. The knife arched dangerously up in the air and plummeted toward the ground. At the last minute Phil held out his hand and the blade sank into the melon.

"Fabulous!" Amanda cried as the audience cheered.

A loud commotion broke out down the hall behind them. "Hey, you can't come in here," the stage manager shouted as he struggled to keep the door closed. There was a splintering sound and the two punks burst into the corridor.

"We're stuck," Amanda breathed. "There's no way out."

On the stage there was a burst of applause as Phil took his bows. Mick took one look at the thugs pounding down the hall and grabbed her hand. "Yes, there is. Come on. It's showtime."

Mick pulled Amanda firmly into the middle of the stage, all the while waving at the crowd. A startled Phil Wilayto looked up in shock as his applause turned to wolf whistles. Out of the corner of her eye, Amanda could see their pursuers prowling behind the black curtains.

"Hey, you're stealing my applause," Phil snapped under his breath. "The next act isn't supposed to come on until . . ." Phil squinted at his unexpected guests.

Mick raised his sunglasses. "It's me. Mick." He pointed to Amanda. "And Mandy."

Phil did a double take at Amanda's appearance. "What are you two doing—"

"Just roll with it, Phil," Mick whispered under

his breath. "We're in trouble." He gestured with his thumb offstage. "Those guys are after us."

Meanwhile the applause had died down and the audience was getting restless. Amanda could hear scraping sounds as the patrons shifted in their seats, and there were a few scattered boos.

"Do something, honey!" a man shouted from the audience. He started clapping in rhythm and the rest of the crowd joined him.

"Phil," Mick hissed. "Juggle."

"No way," Phil answered back. "They want to hear from Mandy."

Mick turned to Amanda and whispered, "Sing a song."

"What song?"

Someone in the back shouted, "Give 'em the hook!"

Amanda wanted to turn and run but when she faced the wings she saw that the punks were poised to grab her the minute she left the stage. She faced the jeering crowd and started singing the first thing that came into her head.

"La, la, la, la, la bamba," she croaked. Her mind went blank, and Amanda cut to the only other words she knew, *"Arriba, arriba!"* She added some dance movements, hoping the audience wouldn't notice that she had no idea what came next.

The piano player and drummer in the pit started playing along loudly and Phil and Mick joined in on the chorus, clapping their hands.

Mick danced up to Amanda and sang, "Let's-get-out-of-here, la bamba!"

"Where-should-we-go, la bamba?" Amanda sang back.

Phil, who was doing a comic impression of a flamenco dancer, cut in, "Follow-me-offstage, la bamba, and-we'll-go-out-the-front, la bamba!"

Phil hopped off the stage and Amanda and Mick were hot on his heels. They did an impromptu conga line through the audience, singing at the top of their lungs. The audience shouted "La bamba!" right along with them.

It only took a few seconds for them to reach the front door but it felt like an eternity. As soon as they were on the street, Mick bellowed, "Run!"

Phil stood his ground. "I'm not running anywhere until someone tells me what's going on."

"Somebody's after us," Mick said, grabbing Phil's arm, "and it's all your fault."

"My fault?" Phil repeated.

Amanda, who'd been keeping watch on the door, shouted, "We can't talk here. We've got to hide." She pointed to the City Lights bookstore across the street. "Let's go there."

Mick spotted a break in the traffic and shouted, "Come on!"

They looped their arms through Phil's and pulled him across the street and through the door of the bookstore. A clerk seated behind the cash register looked up in surprise.

Thinking quickly, Amanda said, "Do you have any books on vacation getaways?"

The clerk nodded and pointed to the stairs. "In the basement."

"Perfect," Mick whispered to Amanda.

They clattered down the steps just as their pursuers flashed by the front window.

"Okay, Phil," Mick said, pulling him behind a row of bookshelves. "I want some answers, and I want them *now.*"

CHAPTER FOURTEEN

"The reason I've missed so much work," Phil explained as the three of them huddled between the bookshelves at City Lights, "is because I've been trying out my act."

Mick squinted at Phil skeptically. "In the afternoon?"

"That's the best time," Phil replied. "That way, the clubs don't lose any business if you bomb."

Amanda crossed her arms and leaned forward. "Then what were you doing making deliveries for J and L Office Supply?"

Phil tilted his head. "All the riders have delivered for that outfit."

"Really?" Amanda asked.

"Yeah. Including Mick," Phil added.

"It's true." Mick narrowed his eyes at Phil. "But I wasn't delivering drugs."

"Drugs?" Phil fell back onto a step stool in the aisle. "Is that what you think I've been doing?"

Mick nodded grimly.

"How can you *say* that?"

"We found twenty thousand dollars' worth of cocaine in a delivery *you* were supposed to make," Amanda hissed.

"Instead, you had Tyrone fill in for you," Mick continued, "and when the drugs weren't delivered, the crooks went after him."

"You should see his face." Amanda winced and shook her head. "He looks awful."

Phil paled visibly and stood up. "But I had no idea what was in that package."

"Come on," Mick scoffed.

"I never look inside," Phil insisted. "Do you?"

"Of course not," Mick replied. "It's against the rules."

"Besides," Phil added, "if I was making so much money dealing drugs, why would I ask for an advance on my salary?"

"Why *did* you?" Mick cut in.

"I needed the money for my tuxedo." Phil flipped up his black satin lapels. "A classy act needs a classy look."

Phil's explanation sounded reasonable to Amanda, but something else bothered her. "Phil, did anyone from Fleet Street know about your club act?"

He shook his head. "I wanted to keep it a secret till I'd perfected it."

Mick met Amanda's eyes and said, "Then what was Charlie doing at the club yesterday?"

"Don't ask me," Phil replied with a shrug. "He's your cousin. I didn't even know he was there." Phil scratched his head. "I wonder if he liked my act."

Mick sighed impatiently. "I wish I knew what was going on here. First, some guys in a limo give me until midnight tonight to get out of business, then twenty thousand dollars' worth of coke falls out of Tyrone's pack, and now a couple of punks are beating up my riders and chasing us all over San Francisco."

"Yeah, and they're going to notice that they passed us," Amanda observed, eyeing the stairs nervously, "and come back and search the stores. I think we ought to get out of here and out of North Beach while we have the chance."

Mick turned back to Phil. "I think you should stay out of sight until this business is cleared up." Phil started to protest and Mick said, "These guys know you're involved now and may come looking for you."

Phil loosened his tie and gulped. "What are you going to do?"

"Go think." Mick checked his watch. "It's nine o'clock. We've still got three hours to figure this out."

Ten minutes later Amanda and Mick had picked

up her scooter, which she'd parked near the club, and were riding through the streets of San Francisco. As the neon lights of North Beach faded away behind them, Amanda felt the tension drain away from her face. She drove toward an isolated overlook facing the vast waters of the Pacific.

When they got off the scooter, Amanda removed the wig she'd been wearing and stuffed it into her pack. "That's much better," she declared, closing her eyes and shaking out her hair. "I feel like a real person again."

"Me, too." Mick tugged the mustache off his upper lip and slipped it into his coat pocket. "That thing was starting to drive me nuts."

They walked to the edge of the overlook and Amanda perched on the stone wall. Mick stood beside her, his hands jammed in his pockets.

It was a moonless night and the stars glittered above the Golden Gate Bridge. They could see the headlights of the cars crossing it, but there was no sound of traffic at that distance.

"We're surrounded by a million people," Mick said softly. "So why do I feel so alone?"

Amanda was startled by the weary sound in his voice. "What do you mean?"

"While we were driving," he said, "I went over all of the suspects in my head. Phil and Ty could be lying about their alibis, but I doubt it. That means two of the top contenders for dealer-of-the-month are Cynthia—" he paused for a second, then added, "And Gabe."

"Gabe? He's your best friend."

Mick shook his head. "He's been acting so weird, I feel like I don't know him anymore."

"It just doesn't seem possible," Amanda whispered.

"Who else is in a better position to control things? He does a lot of the dispatching."

"So does Cynthia," Amanda reminded him.

"Hell, he and Cynthia could be in this together, for all I know."

"Aren't you forgetting someone?" Amanda asked.

"Who?"

"Charlie Driscoll."

Mick shook his head. "Charlie's only been working at Fleet Street for a week."

Amanda cut him off. "He could have set up his system months in advance, working out of J and L's offices. Let's face it, something strange is going on with him. He lied when we saw him at the café, and then yesterday, he was at The Last Laff when he was supposed to be working for you."

Mick's eyes suddenly widened. "That would explain why those hoods jumped me there."

Amanda cocked her head. "What do you mean?"

"Well, Charlie and I look a lot alike, right?"

Amanda nodded. "I'll say."

Mick started pacing back and forth. "What if those guys followed him to the club and then jumped me thinking I was him?"

Amanda studied Mick's face. "I guess it's possible."

Mick's eyes narrowed and his voice became a harsh rasp. "I'd give anything to have our dealer be Charlie, just for the pleasure of turning him in."

Amanda leaned back at the force of his words. "You really don't like Charlie, do you?"

"I hate him."

Amanda was stunned by Mick's voice, cold and deadly quiet. "Why? What did he ever do to you?"

Mick hesitated for a moment, then sat down on the wall beside her. "It's a long story."

A gust of wind blew in from the ocean, and Amanda hugged her shoulders against the chill. "I'd like to hear it."

"I told you before," Mick began slowly, "I wasn't exactly an angel when I was a kid. But Charlie . . ." He shook his head. "He was hell on wheels."

"What'd he do?"

"Stupid stuff. Smashing windows in vacant buildings. Letting the air out of people's tires. Shoplifting. He was always pushing the limits."

Mick kicked at the gravel with the toe of his shoe.

"Finally one night Charlie crossed over the line. He boosted a car that belonged to an old lady and went joyriding all over the city. He ended up totaling the car on the Pacific Highway. Unfortunately, he was wearing my jacket and witnesses thought it was me."

"No!" Amanda breathed.

"I was arrested for grand theft. I didn't have an alibi."

"What did Charlie do?" Amanda asked.

"He let me take the rap."

"What?"

"Yeah. The jerk skipped town, and I spent six months in juvenile hall."

"Oh, Mick," Amanda said softly, "that's terrible."

There was a long pause and Amanda fought the urge to smooth his hair off his forehead. Then she asked quietly, "So why'd you let him come to work for Fleet Street?

Mick stood up abruptly. "He told me he didn't know I'd been arrested. He said that after the accident he left the city and never looked back."

"Maybe he was telling the truth," Amanda suggested.

Mick shrugged. "Maybe."

"And maybe he is really trying to go straight and has nothing to do with this cocaine business."

"But then that would point the finger back at Gabe or Cynthia." Mick shook his head. "And I'd really hate that."

Amanda stood up and moved to Mick. "You know, there is the possibility that no one at Fleet Street is involved. That some drug dealer chose your business to be his unwitting accomplice."

"I've thought about that," Mick said, looking out over the water. "But why would those heavies lean on me if they weren't certain the operation was being run by someone at Fleet Street?"

Amanda looped her arm in his. "Look, Mick, I really think it's time to go to the police."

He shook his head vehemently. "Those hoods think I'm the leader of some drug ring. What's to stop the cops from thinking that, too?"

"Well, then, what are you planning to do?" Amanda asked, pulling away in frustration. "Walk up to Charlie, Gabe, and Cynthia and say, 'I found this cocaine on the street. Is it yours?' "

Mick stared at her and a grin slowly spread across his face. "Great idea."

"Oh, come on, Mick!" Amanda batted him lightly on the shoulder. "I was being sarcastic."

"Yeah, but I think you've really hit on something. I'll just let our three suspects know that I found a box of supplies from J and L."

"And then what?"

"We'll see which one comes to claim it."

Amanda put her hands on her hips. "And when do you plan to do this?"

"Tonight." Mick was already striding back toward the scooter.

"Tonight? But it's after ten o'clock." Amanda hurried to keep up with him. "Can't it wait until tomorrow?"

Mick looped his leg over the seat and slipped

his helmet on his head. "Those hoods gave me three days, and we've run out of time. If we wait, there might not be a tomorrow. For Fleet Street, or for me."

CHAPTER FIFTEEN

Two blocks from Fleet Street, Mick signaled for Amanda to stop. The streetlamp in front of the Sanchez Grocery had burned out and the entire block looked dark and deserted.

"Cut the engine," he whispered. "We'll walk from here." The two of them pushed the scooter the rest of the way to Fleet Street. Amanda was relieved when Mick unlocked the door to the office and they were safely inside. She could have sworn she'd heard footsteps following them the entire way.

"Let's get this over with," Mick said, flicking on the desk lamp.

Amanda moved away from the door. "I just thought of something. If our suspects take the bait and come for the drugs tonight, we're going to need something that looks like a box from J and L Office Supply."

"Should be easy enough." Mick headed for the curtain at the far side of the room. "I'll see what Gabe's dad has in the store."

"Be careful not to turn on any lights out there," Amanda warned. "Somebody could be watching the building."

"I don't need a light. I know this store like the back of my hand." Mick disappeared through the curtain, and moments later Amanda heard a loud crash, followed by a sharp yelp of pain. Her heart leaped into her throat.

"Mick?" she shouted hoarsely. "Are you okay?"

"I'm fine," Mick replied. His voice had a pinched sound to it. "I think Mr. Sanchez has been doing some remodeling. This cold case was never here before."

"Mick, do you keep a log of all your dispatches?" Amanda called.

"Yes," he answered. "It's in the top right-hand drawer of the desk."

"Do you mind if I go over it?" she asked as she sat in the heavy oak chair. "I think we may have overlooked something."

There was another thunk from the front of the store and Mick shouted, "Go ahead."

Amanda opened the drawer and pulled out the ledger. Something had been plaguing her ever since they had found out J & L was involved in the drug running. She knew how the drugs were being delivered, but how were the orders being placed?

"This should do it," Mick said, holding up a small brown box as he reentered the office. "I filled it with a few bottles of nail polish to give it some weight." He pulled a roll of clear strapping tape out of the desk drawer and taped the top of the box shut.

"Perfect." Amanda nodded her approval.

"Now for the calls." Mick set the box under the desk lamp and picked up the phone. Amanda carried the ledger to the overstuffed couch and listened while Mick dialed the first number.

"Yo, Cyn?" Mick perched on the corner of the desk as he spoke. "I was wondering if you'd do me a big favor? I'm going to be out of the office tomorrow morning, so would you mind opening up? I'll leave the key in the usual place. Oh, and by the way . . ." He ran his finger along the edge of the cardboard box. "I found a box from J and L Office Supply that didn't get delivered. Tyrone must've dropped it on the floor. Could you return it tomorrow? I'll leave it on the desk by the phone." There was a short pause and then Mick said, "Thanks, Cyn, I really appreciate this. See you in the afternoon."

Mick hung up the phone and looked at Amanda. "How'd I do?"

"You sounded great," Amanda replied with an encouraging smile. As Mick dialed the second number, Amanda focused her attention on the ledger.

Each page was divided into four columns listing the name of the business that requested a messenger, the name of the messenger sent on the call, the time and place of pickup, and the time and place of delivery.

Mick's call to his cousin was almost identical to the one he had made to Cynthia, but there was a hard edge in his voice that Amanda now understood. Mick hung up the phone and shoved it away from him.

"Aren't you going to call Gabe?" Amanda asked, looking up from the ledger.

Mick shook his head. "I don't have the heart. I'm just going to hope that it's not him."

Amanda shut the ledger and stood up. "So what do we do now?"

"We wait." Mick dug into the bottom drawer of the desk and pulled out a small flashlight. He flicked off the desk lamp, grabbed a couple of cushions off the couch, and gestured toward the storeroom. "We'll hide in here."

Amanda had barely made it into the storeroom when the door to the alley rattled. Mick turned off the flashlight and cracked the door slightly. The two of them held their breaths as a figure switched on the overhead light.

"Gabe!" Mick moaned softly. Amanda could guess how betrayed Mick felt and she squeezed his hand in sympathy.

They stood quietly behind the door and watched Gabe take off his heavy jacket and toss it over a chair. He crossed to the couch and pulled out a canvas bag. Amanda remembered seeing him put it there earlier that day.

Mick burst out of the storeroom. "Give me that bag!"

Gabe was so startled, he dropped the bag and instantly assumed a martial arts fighting stance. Every muscle in his body was tensed like a coiled spring, ready to explode. He blinked several times and finally choked out, "Mick? What're you trying to do, scare me to death?"

Mick moved stiffly toward his friend. "I said, give me the bag."

"What's your problem?" Gabe asked, stepping back.

Mick stuck out his hand. "Give it to me."

Looking totally confused, Gabe murmured, "Take it easy, man." He picked up the canvas bag and tossed it in Mick's direction. "You want it, you can have it."

Without answering, Mick pulled open the bag and stared inside. Then he looked back at Gabe and stammered, "Th-these—these are *books*!"

"Yeah," Gabe said, yanking the bag out of Mick's hands. "Schoolbooks. What'd you think was in there? Drugs?"

"Well, I, uh . . ." Mick looked back at Amanda for help.

She stepped out of the storeroom and said, "That's what he thought."

"What!" Gabe's jaw fell open. "I never touch that stuff." He turned on Mick. "You know that."

"Well, yeah, I do," Mick blustered. "But . . ."

"But what?" Gabe challenged.

"Mick had to be sure," Amanda said, moving between the two boys. "You see, we discovered that someone's been using Fleet Street to run drugs in the financial district."

Gabe gave a low whistle, then looked at Mick, his face full of hurt. "But that's no reason to suspect me."

Amanda crossed her arms and said gently, "You must admit, you've been acting a little strange lately."

"That reminds me," Mick cut in, "what are you doing with schoolbooks, anyway?"

Gabe smiled. "Going to school."

Mick ran one hand through his hair. "Come again?"

"You've always said I should finish high school. I finally took your advice." Gabe set the canvas bag on the desk and patted it proudly. "I've been studying for my G.E.D."

"At night school?"

Gabe nodded.

"But why didn't you tell me?" Mick asked.

Gabe looked at the floor sheepishly. "I didn't want to make a big deal about it. You know . . ." He shrugged. "In case I didn't pass."

"When's your final?" Amanda asked.

"I took it this morning."

"And?" Mick and Amanda both leaned forward expectantly.

"I aced the sucker." Gabe's face spread into a wide grin. He looped his fingers under his suspenders and strutted around the desk. "You two are looking at a genuine high school graduate."

"Gabe, that's fantastic!" Amanda clapped her hands together.

Mick lunged forward and wrapped his arms around his friend. "You lousy bum," he crowed, "congratulations!"

The two boys pounded each other on the back. Then Gabe suddenly pushed Mick away from him. "I should be angry with you. How could you think I was dealing drugs?"

"Sorry, man," Mick said, clapping his friend on the shoulder. "But so much has happened to me during the last four days, I'd suspect my own mother."

Amanda checked her watch and gasped. "Mick, it's almost midnight."

"What happens at midnight?" Gabe asked.

"We're out of business—permanently," Mick replied. "Unless we receive a visitor real soon."

Gabe raised an eyebrow. "You'd better fill me in."

Mick quickly explained their plan while Amanda grabbed Gabe's coat and turned off the light. Mick was so busy talking, they almost didn't hear the key as it clicked quietly in the front door. They didn't even have time to get to the storeroom. Amanda dove behind the couch while Mick and Gabe crouched beside a stack of boxes, hiding from the intruder.

The door opened, and a slender beam of a light sliced through the darkness. A soft padding of footsteps followed the beam over to the desk. The light focused on the cardboard box, then a hand flicked on the desk lamp, revealing the face of the intruder.

"Aha!" Mick sprang to his feet. "I knew it had to be you."

CHAPTER SIXTEEN

Charlie Driscoll looked up in surprise, the cardboard box marked J & L Office Supply held firmly in his hands. A smile creased his face and he cracked, "Hey, guys. Working late?"

"Very funny." Mick cast a steely gaze at his cousin as Gabe and Amanda got to their feet. Gabe moved to the door, blocking Charlie's escape, while Mick knocked the box out of Charlie's hand and confronted his cousin.

"How long have you been working for J and L?" Mick demanded.

Charlie looked perplexed. "What are you talking about?"

"You've been using Fleet Street to run drugs in the financial district."

"You're not serious?" Charlie said, trying to laugh it off.

Mick grabbed his cousin and shoved him up against the wall. "Don't mess with me, Charlie. I don't like being used."

Charlie's face suddenly changed and he said, "Look, Mick, you've got it all wrong. I've been—"

Mick's hands tightened on Charlie's collar. "I was doing just fine until you came back into my life, and now you're trying to drag me down again."

"But—"

"Charlie, you're in over your head," Mick shouted in his cousin's face. "You stepped on the toes of a much bigger organization and those guys want to shut you down for good."

"What guys?" Charlie asked.

"I don't know." Mick shook his head in exasperation. "Tough guys in overcoats and limos who don't take kindly to you cutting in on their territory. I don't care what you do with your own life, but by using Fleet Street to take orders and make deliveries, you've put us all in danger."

A light suddenly went on in Amanda's head. "The orders," she shouted, snapping her fingers.

Amanda rushed back into the storage room, where she'd left the ledger, and flipped open the pages till she came to the most recent orders. She nodded with satisfaction. "It was here all the time, and I just never saw it."

She ran to the door. "Mick, we've made a terrible mistake."

Mick still held Charlie firmly against the wall. He looked over his shoulder at her. "What?"

"It's not Charlie, after all."

"What do you mean? We caught him red-handed."

Amanda carried the ledger over to Mick and Gabe and lay it open on top of a stack of crates. "Look, we know that all your riders made deliveries *from* J and L, but according to your records, nobody ever took any orders *to* J and L."

"So?" Mick shrugged. "Maybe Charlie got another messenger service to handle that part of the operation."

"No, you don't get it." Amanda pushed her hair off of her face. "My very first day on the job, I remember dropping off an order to J and L, but look here." She pointed to the ledger. "There's no record of it. Then, the very next day, I saw one of your messengers drop a piece of paper; it was an order for office supplies from J and L. The order was for three boxes of paper clips."

"Just three?" Gabe asked. "That's weird."

"Exactly." Amanda slammed her hand down on the ledger in disgust. "I should have trusted my instincts. Why would anyone go to the expense of hiring a messenger just to deliver a simple order like that?"

"Unless that order was a code for something else," Mick cut in.

"What do you mean?" Gabe asked.

"Like, three boxes of paper clips could mean," Mick said slowly, "three grams of cocaine."

Amanda nodded. "Right."

Charlie had stopped resisting and was listening intently to their conversation. Gabe pointed to him. "But how does this let Charlie off the hook?"

Amanda shut the ledger with a resounding slam. "Because the person who dropped that order was the same person who delivered a message to J and L my first day of work—a delivery that was never recorded."

"Who was that?" Gabe demanded.

They heard the click of a gun behind them and a voice said quietly, "Me."

Amanda nearly jumped out of her skin. She spun around with the others and stared at the slim figure standing in the doorway.

"Cynthia!" Mick rasped. "I don't believe it."

"Sorry, Mickey," she said with a cold smile, "but it's true." Cynthia pointed the barrel of her steel-gray pistol straight at them. "Everybody, put your hands where I can see them, and line up against the wall."

The four of them did as they were ordered. "Oh, and Mick?" She motioned toward the cardboard box lying between them on the floor. "Why don't you just hand me the merchandise there—very slowly—and then I'll just disappear."

Amanda watched Mick pick up the box and walk

stiffly over to Cynthia. He looked as if he were sleepwalking. All he said was, "Why?"

Cynthia shrugged. "For the money. What else?" Then she laughed. "And because it was so easy."

Amanda saw the hurt register on Mick's smooth features. Cynthia had used him to serve her own purposes, had abused his trust, and for that Amanda hated her.

Cynthia backed up to the desk, keeping the pistol trained on the foursome. She started to open the box and Amanda flashed a silent warning to Mick. Cynthia was about to discover that the cocaine wasn't in the box. Amanda leaped forward. "You'll never get away with this."

"Of course I will," Cynthia said confidently.

She tugged at the tape on the box and Amanda shouted, "Not after we tell the police about you and J and L."

"Don't bother. As of tonight, there is no J and L—just an empty room. It'll be your word against mine."

Cynthia set the box down as she perched on the edge of the desk. "They can't trace any of this to me," she gloated. "Check the ledger. You'll notice I never delivered any of the drugs. I made sure of that." She smiled at Mick. "All the evidence points to you and your riders."

Mick didn't respond but stared back at her dully.

"Oh, by the way." Cynthia moved to her locker and threw open the metal door. She took out a sweatshirt and a pair of bicycle clips. "I'm giving my notice."

She picked up the little box off the desk and tucked it under her arm. "My associates will be glad to see this."

Amanda narrowed her eyes at Cynthia. "You mean, those two punks who beat up Tyrone?"

"That was too bad about Ty," Cynthia said, flipping up the hood of her black windbreaker and backing toward the door. "Give him my apologies, will you?"

"Mick, do something!" Amanda hissed under her breath. "She's getting away."

"What do you want me to do?" he mumbled out of the corner of his mouth.

"I don't know," Amanda replied. "Just—"

Suddenly the door behind Cynthia burst open and crashed against the wall. Two burly men in dark suits brandishing snub-nosed revolvers stepped into the room. Amanda recognized them as the ones who had attacked them in the alley.

"You had your chance," one of them snarled at Mick. "We gave you till midnight to shut down your operation."

The shorter of the two added, "Time's up."

As the hoods advanced on Mick, he shouted, "You're barking up the wrong tree." He pointed at Cynthia, who had fallen back against the lockers. "She's the wheeler-dealer here."

The two men turned on Cynthia, who pointed her pistol at them shakily. "He's lying!"

"Come *on,* Cyn," Mick growled. "Why don't you tell them what you told us?"

"Yeah, *chica,*" Gabe spoke up. "Tell them how you used Fleet Street to do the dirty work for you and your friends at J and L."

"That's not true." Cynthia still held the cardboard box tightly under one arm. She struggled to cover it with the jacket of her windbreaker.

"If you don't believe us," Mick said, "ask her what's in the box."

"Shut up," Cynthia hissed at Mick. "There's nothing in here."

Mick shrugged. "Twenty thousand dollars' worth of cocaine is a lot of nothing."

"Okay, little girl, quit playing around." The taller of the hoods moved slowly toward her. "Drop the gun, and hand over the box."

Cynthia's face was a tight mask of anger. "You want it?" Her voice cracked in her throat. "Catch!"

The cardboard box hit the man in the chest and burst open. Bottles of nail polish fell out and rolled across the floor. He stared down at them in astonishment. "What the—"

Cynthia shot Mick a look of pure hatred, then bolted for the open door. The man lunged at her, tackling her around the waist. Cynthia's gun clattered to the floor in front of the desk and Mick dove for it.

"Don't touch that gun!" The other man aimed his revolver at Mick.

Charlie, who had stood quietly by during the

entire confrontation, suddenly threw himself between them. A shot rang out and Charlie howled in pain.

Above all of the commotion a voice bellowed from the doorway, "Police! Freeze!"

CHAPTER SEVENTEEN

Amanda was never so relieved to see a policeman in her entire life. Sergeant Rubano stood in the doorway, holding a bullhorn. What seemed like a full company of blue-coated policemen stood behind him, their guns trained on the people inside.

The sergeant gestured at the two men and commanded, "Take these guys out in the alley and frisk 'em." A pair of officers quickly hustled the two hoods out of the room.

Cynthia crawled slowly on her hands and knees over to the curtain leading into the grocery store.

"Cynthia Spartaro!"

The sergeant's voice stopped her cold. The fear on her face made her look like a little girl.

"Cynthia Spartaro, you're under arrest on charges of conspiring to sell illicit drugs."

Cynthia's chin began to quiver as a patrolman sprang forward and pulled her to her feet.

"Take her outside," the sergeant commanded. "And don't forget to read her her rights."

Mick knelt beside his cousin, who lay clutching his thigh on the floor. A dark pool of blood was forming near his knee.

"Mandy, get the first-aid kit," Mick rasped. "It's in the first locker by the door."

"We may need more bandages," Gabe muttered. "I'll get some from inside the store." He stood up and hurried through the curtain.

Amanda grabbed the white metal box and carried it over to Mick, who'd propped Charlie up into a sitting position and was examining his wound. He took a roll of gauze from Amanda and hurriedly pressed it against the bleeding wound.

Mick stared at his cousin, a strange expression on his face. "You saved my life," he said finally. "Thanks."

Charlie winced as Mick, using a pair of scissors from the first-aid kit, carefully cut his pantleg away from the wound. "It was nothing."

"It was more than nothing." Mick sat back on his heels. "It was stupid. What made you jump in the line of fire like that?"

Charlie forced a smile. "You took the rap for me two years ago. I figured the least I could do was take a bullet for you."

Amanda watched as a confused jumble of emotions passed over Mick's face. He swallowed hard, then jerked his head toward the policeman by the door. "An ambulance," Mick shouted in a choked voice. "My cousin needs an ambulance!"

"The paramedics are on the way," Sergeant Rubano said, coming up behind them. Then to everyone's surprise the detective knelt down and put his hand on Charlie's shoulder. "You okay, Driscoll?"

"Yeah, Sarge." Then Charlie added with a grin, "It's only a scratch."

Mick sat up with a start. "You two know each other?"

"Yeah." Charlie gestured with his thumb to the burly policeman. "This is my boss."

"Sergeant Rubano?" Mick and Amanda gasped at the same time.

Charlie chuckled. "Yeah, he's responsible for keeping me straight."

"Whoa, back up a minute." Mick ran his hand through his thick hair and then squinted at his cousin. "Are you telling me that you're a *cop*?"

"Brilliant deduction, Sherlock." Charlie patted Mick on the shoulder.

"Then what are you doing working for me?" Mick demanded.

"I asked Charlie to go undercover for us," Sergeant Rubano explained. "The IRS alerted us that something illegal was going on at J and L Office

Supply, so we put them under surveillance several months ago."

"When we found out your outfit was handling all of their deliveries," Charlie continued, "the sarge decided we needed a man on a bike." Charlie grinned at Mick. "Me. I told them you wouldn't be too keen about taking me on. Not after what happened two years ago."

"I wanted to slam the door in your face," Mick admitted. "But we were shorthanded. And . . ." He stared at his hands. "You *are* my cousin."

"Sarge?" a patrolman called from the doorway. Flashing blue and red lights lit up the alley behind him.

"What is it?"

The patrolman held up the broken cardboard box. "Is this where the dope was supposed to be? There's nothing here but a few bottles of nail polish."

"I thought there was cocaine in there," Rubano exclaimed.

"Excuse me, Sergeant Rubano," Amanda interrupted, "but the evidence you're looking for is locked away in my uncle's safe at home."

"Does anyone else know it's there?" Rubano asked worriedly.

"Just Mick and me," Amanda replied. Then she snapped her fingers and added, "And one more person. My best friend, Pepper. But she doesn't really know what it is."

"What do you mean by that?" The detective

stared at Amanda for a moment, scratching his head.

"It's a long story, but it doesn't matter because she's skiing up at Tahoe."

"Well, as soon as the ambulance gets here," the sergeant said, "I'm going to want all of you to come down to headquarters. I'll need to take your statements." He helped Amanda to her feet. "We'll swing by your house along the way and pick up the evidence." He turned back to Charlie and smiled. "In the meantime, nice detective work, Driscoll. We seemed to have gotten two birds with one stone." He nodded toward the door. "Those two work for Sid Candino."

"Candino?" Mick choked.

Out in the alley Amanda could see the two thugs being hustled into a waiting squad car. "Who's that?" she asked in a whisper.

"He's the syndicate's boss in San Francisco." Gabe whistled softly. "Not many people mess with Sid Candino and live to tell about it."

Mick turned to Amanda, who suddenly felt queasy. "Believe me, I had no idea Candino was mixed up in this," he said. "I would never have gotten you involved."

Amanda thought of all the times Mick had risked his life for her and she whispered huskily, "I'm glad you did."

A wailing siren signaled the arrival of the ambulance. Two men in white coats came into the room, carrying a stretcher. As they strapped Charlie onto it, Sergeant Rubano said, "I can't thank you enough." He clasped Charlie's hand firmly. "You did the department proud. I'll see you get a commendation from the superintendent."

"Wait a minute," Charlie protested. "Don't thank me. I didn't crack this case."

The sergeant looked confused. "Then who did?"

Charlie gestured to Mick and Amanda. "Hart and Soul."

Sergeant Rubano's eyes widened in surprise. Mick slipped his arm around Amanda's waist and the two of them beamed proudly at the detective.

"And, if you ask me," Charlie called as the paramedics wheeled him out the door, "they make one hell of a team."

On Monday morning Amanda stood in the main hall of Sutter Academy and sighed. It didn't seem possible that spring break was already over. So much had happened in that short week.

"Mandy!" Pepper's familiar voice rang down the corridor behind her. "Wait up!"

Amanda's jaw fell open as she watched her redheaded friend hobble through the front entrance of Sutter. Her left leg was encased in a plaster cast that stretched from her toe up to her hip. Pepper raised a crutch and brandished it at the students who had stopped to gape at her.

"One smart remark out of any of you," she warned, "and I'll break this over your head." Laughter broke out among the kids as they moved aside to let her pass. Pepper limped up to her friend.

Pepper caught the look in Amanda's eye and declared, "Don't say it. I don't want to hear it."

"But what happened?" Amanda exclaimed.

Pepper glanced over both shoulders, then whispered, "I didn't do this skiing. I slipped getting out of the car in the parking lot at Tahoe."

"What?"

"I never even put on a pair of ski boots," Pepper said bitterly. "I spent the entire vacation in the lodge."

"Oh, Pepper, that's terrible." Amanda started to giggle and Pepper snapped, "Go ahead and laugh, but I don't find this very funny."

She waved her crutch again and Amanda covered her mouth to stop laughing. "I'm sorry, it's just that you had such high hopes of meeting Mr. Wonderful on the slopes, and now . . ."

"I know, I know." Pepper leaned on her crutch and shoved her glasses up on her nose. "Maybe next year. In the meantime, I did meet a couple of cute waiters and a guy who's even clumsier than I am. He broke *both* legs slipping on a ham sandwich in the snack bar."

"You're kidding!" This time Amanda was laughing uncontrollably.

"No, I'm not," Pepper retorted. "And here's the really incredible part—we both have the same orthopedist." Pepper smiled coyly. "This Friday,

Ted and I are going for a date after our doctor's appointments."

"So everything worked out after all," Amanda said.

"Yeah," Pepper admitted with a grin. "But enough about me. How was your week? What finally happened with Fleet Street?"

Amanda opened her mouth to reply but stopped when she spotted something taped to the door of her locker. It was a manila envelope with five words written on the outside:

To My Long Stemmed Rose

A warm feeling surged through Amanda as she tore open the envelope. A small photograph, clipped out of the *San Francisco Chronicle*, fell into her hand. Pepper hobbled behind her to peer at the picture.

"Hey, that's you and Mick with Sergeant Rubano!"

Amanda smiled and nodded. She and Mick stood side by side in the police station looking tired, but happy. They'd spent nearly two hours answering questions, and afterward Mick had taken her to his favorite late-night spot for supper. The date had been perfect. Mick was his charming, funny self again. The dinner was the best she'd ever tasted. And their kiss . . .

Amanda blinked as Pepper took the clipping and read the caption out loud. "Local teens

Amanda Hart and Mickey Soul help SFPD crack drug ring." Pepper's eyes widened and she almost dropped one of her crutches. "Police? Drug ring?" She stared back at the picture. "And *what* is *that* you're wearing?"

The photo showed Amanda still clad in the red satin sheath, complete with the rhinestone straps and revealing side slit. "That's the costume I wore for my act at the comedy club."

"What act?" Pepper fell back against the lockers in amazement. "What club?"

Amanda sighed wearily. "It's a long story."

"Tell me about it." Pepper tapped her knuckles against her cast. "I've got all the time in the world." Pepper narrowed her eyes at her friend. "And I want to know every teensy-weensy, juicy detail. Starting *now*."

ABOUT THE AUTHOR

JAHNNA N. MALCOLM is really the pen name for a husband-and-wife team, Jahnna Beecham and Malcolm Hillgartner. Together they have written twenty-one books, including five titles for Bantam's Sweet Dreams series under the name Jahnna Beecham. Both are professional actors and have trod the boards in theatres across the United States and Europe. In fact, they met at an audition and were married on the stage. Jahnna and Malcolm live in Montana with their son, Dashiell McLean, and their old dog, Clarence.